T0051593

CLASH
FICTION

Cover art and interior by Joel Amat Güell
joelamatguell.com | *@joelamatguell*

ISBN: 9781955904933

Troy, NY
CLASH Books
clashbooks.com

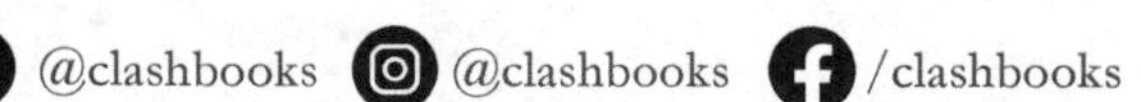

@clashbooks @clashbooks /clashbooks

Email: clashmediabooks@gmail.com

Juliet Escoria

WITCH HUNT
& BLACK CLOUD

NEW AND SELECTED WORKS

Introduction *by* Scott McClanahan

I've been trying to write this introduction for some time now, but I keep failing. I keep telling myself, "Quit spending so much time on it. It's just an introduction." But it's hard to work out what I want to say about these books.

So I'll start again.

Some biographical facts:

Juliet Escoria was born in Australia in 1982 and spent her childhood in southern California.

Juliet Escoria is not Juliet Escoria's real name.

In her youth, two young women were murdered in two separate incidents on the beach in front of her house. Since then, the beach has been the site of numerous assaults, accidents, and fatalities (often involving off-duty police officers). Juliet Escoria is still afraid to walk on this beach at night.

Her mother and father were skydivers. At one jump, a woman's chute wouldn't open, and she was killed upon impact. When it happened, the woman's husband and family were all watching from the jump-site. A young Escoria was watching too.

She started writing bad poetry as a teenager and spent time institutionalized following two suicide attempts. She was diagnosed as bipolar. These events are chronicled in her novel, *Juliet the Maniac.*

During her teenage years, she developed a problem with drugs and alcohol. Often with friends, she engaged in drunken prank phone calls, which sometimes involved calling Gateway Computer's Customer service. They once complained about bringing home a brand-new computer and finding a KKK hat in their Gateway Computer box. They were so righteous in their outrage that they almost got a free computer out of it.

From 2009-2011, Juliet Escoria moved to New York and attended Brooklyn College. She studied with Amy Hempel and Jenny Offill. She worked on her writing.

She got sober with the help of a certain 12-step program.

For several years during grad school, she covered readings for the blog at Electric Literature. These are classics of internet reportage. She met everyone.

At one event, she asked Don DeLillo if she could take his picture for the blog.

Don DeLillo responded, "No."

Juliet Escoria politely replied, "Well, thanks for humoring me, Mr. DeLillo."

Don DeLillo responded, "I wasn't humoring you."

But perhaps these disparate events are somehow important.

About Black Cloud:

I first met Juliet Escoria at a small reading in Brooklyn. During that time, she was already at work on the stories that would make up her first collection, *Black Cloud.* The book was published in 2014 on a small press that no longer exists. On the cover of the book was a picture of her face. Inside its pages, were pictures of her body.

There were stories about anger and spite, resentment and confusion, fear and disgust and revenge. But they were all short and seductive. The sentences crackled. She created a persona for herself that I've often seen imitated since.

In the first year we were married, I went to pick up her medicine at the drugstore. The pharmacist asked her name.

I said, "Juliet Escoria."

The woman looked it up on the computer, but the name wasn't there.

I suddenly realized my mistake. I'd called her by her pen name rather than her real name.

I tried to explain this to the pharmacist, but in the middle of the opioid epidemic, the pharmacist treated me like a criminal. She said, "So your wife has an alias?"

I kept repeating, "No a pen name. A pen name."

I laughed when I got home. I had mixed these two people up in my mind. The character Juliet Escoria, and the woman who wrote about her. Strangely, I was married to them both.

About Witch Hunt:

In 2014-2015, she was struggling to write the novel that became *Juliet the Maniac*. The last time she tried to write this book was in 2013, and it was also the last time she was hospitalized. In 2014-15, I listened to her ranting about how much she hated poetry, how much she hated poets. She turned her frustration into the poetry collection *Witch Hunt*. It was published by a small press that no longer exists.

Witch Hunt is maybe my favorite of her books. In its anti-poetry, she did new things. She made fun of other poems, she stomped on poems. She included a whole section about how much she hated horses. It was almost as if the book solely existed as an exercise for uniting horse-haters across the world.

If I break my leg, I just go to the doctor. If you do it, you're dead.

This isn't a joke, I really do hate horses, they should all just die.

It's perhaps the only poems in all of American literature dedicated to how awful horses can be, a breakthrough for those who hate certain animals everywhere.

It's hard to remember the way the internet once was. But both of these books will take their rightful place in that small canon known as "internet literature." Juliet Escoria is older now, but I still remember the young woman who once wrote these books. I am older too. You would be shocked by how kind she is in real life, how loyal a friend, how loving a step-mother.

She is at work now on a book about the murders that happened in front of her house. It's unlike anything she has ever done. She sharpening her knives and preparing to kill off the writer she once was. A writer always *is*, never *was*. She is busy making herself new.

But when I re-read these books, I feel as if I am holding the writer I first fell in love with.

Turn the page, and you can hold her too.

TABLE OF CONTENTS

for Scott

WITCH HUNT

I

AXL ROSE AND OTHER MEN

Whatever Useless Things

When he kissed
me there was only
one more thing
I wanted and that
was to completely
disappear.
The mornings left
my insides sore
and the outer part
of me in a dust
film broken
pieces of skin
and no dreams
remembered.
He did not regret
his wanting
although he
may have regretted
the fulfillment
but what else
is there
to say about
desire.
The answer is
disappointing.
The answer is
not much.

David Foster Wallace's Rock Idol Was Axl Rose

In the music video for "November Rain,"
Axl marries and then kills off his
in-real-life girlfriend Stephanie Seymour.
I think you'd have to not much believe
in the power of your magic,
or whatever you want to call it,
to do something so stupid like that.

But maybe Axl was aware and just didn't care,
just wanted to see what he was fucking with.
Maybe he wanted Stephanie to be dead,
incapable of letting anyone but him
love her ever again.
Maybe he wanted her beautiful body
to rot away,
maybe he knew that we all look
the same
when we've been dead for long enough.

Anyway, she didn't die
so maybe Axl just isn't that good
at magic.
Instead of marriage or death,
they just assaulted and sued
each other a couple of times
which I guess is a
lesser kind of marriage,
a lesser kind of death.

Emotional Truth

Axl Rose is wearing
tight leggings patterned in roses
his penis popping large as a
tube sock
body shaking on the
sexy psychologist's recliner
in a way that seems too ridiculous
to ever happen in real life
except VH1's Behind the Music said
he was undergoing intensive therapy
at the time of that music video
so maybe that's the way to dress
if you want to heal.
Maybe I'm doing it
wrong.

Lose My Delusion

His hair was a puddle
on fire wet for
slippage burning for
slickness and there was
a reason he married
only the once. Hips
don't lie, a wise man
once said, and his
were no
exception because
under his jeans I found
truth.

Angels drowned
beneath his skin it is
their light with which
he remembers it is
their light which allows
him to forget
Indiana because
if that didn't happen
then how could one
truly inhabit
those shorts besides
everyone knows
geniuses don't grow
in the Midwest,
just corn.

Today's Tarot Spread

I do not know your fate but
I am certain it does not involve
loving me.
Just wanted to let you know.
Figured it might make you happy.
Maybe not now but
in the long run.

Wild West

"Cowboy Song"
is about a Black
Irishman
who wants to tame
some ponies
and I think I'm the kind of girl
who could let him

I'd take him on a quiet ride
down into the dirt
show him how there is a place
on the horizon where everything
bleeds the same same same

Oh but when it storms
the thunder claps
box your ears with
violence
it will witch you away
if you are not careful
it will make your
nose bleed

the thing they never told him
back on the other side of the world
is what happens when the cowboying
goes wrong

I remember a ranch house with two
cowboy sons
the younger did heroin and
it got real bad until
one day the older found him
dangling from the rafters

years later the voices spoke
and paranoia lifted him
he took a rifle and blew apart
his head
there were spiders in the walls
the sunsets blew out trails of bats
and everything was
just how he imagined

we drank from two glasses of
ice cold Coca-Cola
I made a promise about
transferring money into
his bank
but the truth is
there are only three things
you can do with a man like that:
forgive,
forget,
throw away.

Roman Candle

Listening to Elliott Smith
reminds me of the time
I was girlfriend to a junkie
and we lived in darkness
except for afternoon trips to a diner
where he nodded out over eggs
and I felt mortified each time
even though most meals
were interrupted by me running to the bathroom
to vomit.

At some point we changed places
but I didn't notice until
I was on top of mailboxes
a block away from my apartment
because I had fallen asleep again
while driving.

29th Street, Manhattan

The best catcall I ever
received
started out regular,
with the man saying,
Hey baby.

I had just left my therapist
where I started
crying uncontrollably
in the middle, and left
feeling shaky
and split open,

so I was in no mood.

He was with his friends
and changed his
tune so fast:
calling me stank ass,
and that no one wanted
me anyway,
that I needed
to eat some chicken
and eggs.

I think maybe he meant
steak.

I yelled at him
to fuck off, faggot—
a thing I would not
normally say but
it had the

desired effect.

I got onto the subway
before something
worse could happen.
I never went back
to that therapist.
She called me several times,
wondering if I was OK,
but it seemed impossible
to call back
or pick up the phone.

Casual Misandry

Maybe I would write about
Cocks
If they weren't so
Stupid
If they didn't
Resemble dumb
Noses waggling in the
Air
They're not like
Vaginas
Complicated
And interesting
They are just
Billy clubs
Mistaken by
Blind people
For guns.

Here is a joke I know:
Gentlemen,
Look in your
Trousers.

Here is another:
Q. How many
Cocks
Does it take
To change a
Lightbulb?
A. Zero
Because
They're
None
Too
Bright.

Just The Tip

When
Writing
Poem
It
Best
To
Be
Hungry
Although
Not
Always
For
Food

Letters To Ex-Lovers

DEAR ROBERT,

I'm not sorry for forgetting your address, your phone number, or even your name, but I must admit I do have some regrets about the loss of your face. When I think of you there is nothing anymore, just static.

So I don't remember what you looked like the day you took me down to the beach, how your voice sounded, what you said. I do remember there was no one around and your hands were hot and sticky. I remember how it seemed like something bad would happen later and it did. I never meant for it to escalate that way, I just wanted you to stop yelling. I was picking glass shards out of the carpeting of my car for weeks.

DEAR CHRISTOPHER,

I wore blue to court, a button-up shirt with ruffles down the front I had bought especially for the occasion. I heard somewhere that blue was the color of innocence. The public defender they assigned me was young and had greasy hair. She seemed sad. You were there, with your mother, so I guess that meant you two were talking again. I didn't want things like that to go well for you. I wanted for your mother to hate you, to see you the way that I saw you. I wanted for you to hate yourself. I wanted for you to die.

The restraining order passed, but I had no proof for the property damage and I had not photographed the bruises. They told me if you violated it, I should call the police, which left me unsure of the restraining order's purpose. But you left me alone from then on out, so I guess it worked.

Sometimes now, a decade later, I still look at your Facebook. For a long time it appeared like you didn't have a job and I hoped it was because I had ruined you, but it seems like you're doing better now. Your string of girlfriends has turned progressively less attractive, a fact I hold on to tightly, because I need some tangible evidence that I won, that you lost, that I beat you.

DEAR SEAN,

I did not want a relationship at the time, but then again I never do. You went to my party. I'd never seen you before but no one had anything bad to say about you, so I let you stay over and after a while you never really left. I would not let you fuck me. I had no good reason for this, I just didn't want to. I couldn't figure out why you stayed around, why you wanted to hold me, why you wanted to sleep in my bed, why I wanted you to. Sometimes the worst thing to be is alone.

One day I came home from work and you were smoking meth on my couch. I didn't get mad. Instead I joined you. We were up for several days. At the end, we had sex and it went poorly, so I locked you out of the apartment when you went for a cigarette. You mistook my neighbor's door for mine and banged on it for over an hour. The police were called. I never saw you again. I felt like I should care, about any of it, but I didn't have any thoughts on the matter either way. I heard you left town after that. Good riddance.

DEAR ELIJAH,

You brought us home after the bar closed and offered to make us some cocktails. The liquor was new, you said, expensive, had notes of berries or butter or something else that made it seem high class, and my friend was interested in that type of thing. I came along because I was feeling agreeable.

I remember falling limp, the embarrassment at the loss of control over my limbs. I woke up later in your bed, the blankets pulled over my body, my clothes folded neatly on the floor, my mouth tasting of vomit. My friend had disappeared, as had yours, and the apartment was silent. You were at the foot of the bed watching sports on mute. There were no lights on.

I don't know what happened in that bed while I was under. Maybe nothing. I would have asked but I didn't know you well enough to phrase it in a way that didn't sound ugly. I did not feel violated, then or the next day or even now. You never caused me pain. The only thing you gave me was a question: What happened during that time, in that space? And if you did something bad, and I never knew about it – does the bad thing have no weight? Does it matter?

DEAR ADAM,

I spent nearly every night with you for a month, but I don't think I ever learned what you cared about. Sometimes you claimed to have spent the day making music, not the real kind but by using a computer. Whenever I asked to hear, you said it wasn't ready.

The only food you ever ate was that prepared by other people. The only thing in your fridge was take-out leftovers, beer, and vegan ice cream. You claimed to care about health, hence the veganism, but I never saw you without a cigarette. You told me once you'd never been in love but spoke so fondly of an ex it was hard to believe you.

I decided to go away for the summer. When I came back the emptiness had gone which meant you'd outlived your purpose. I went over to your apartment anyway. You alluded to having had other relationships while I was away, but your browser history showed too much porn for that, even for you. I never got the chance to hear you speak an honest word. I wonder if that's even something you know how to do.

DEAR THOMAS,

I tried to not judge your drinking but it was hard sometimes. I'd come over and the sun wouldn't even be down and you'd be slurring your words already. By the time I'd had a few, you'd be blacked out, belligerent, yelling about something or another for no reason.

You had so much anger toward your mother. I guess you didn't like the fact that she'd succumbed to cancer, and maybe because your brother hung himself shortly after. You blamed her death for his, which seemed really unfair. You only ever spoke of it when you were drunk so I never understood the logic, or if there was any.

I laughed at you when you ended it, not because of the end but because of your reason: I drank too much. But your next girlfriend was that sweet girl with the high-pitched voice and the love for Jesus. I guess you wanted someone to save you. I will be the first to admit— that was never one of my strengths.

DEAR COLIN,

At that point, you had figured out you were mostly gay but were still experimenting with women. You said you liked me because I was a pinup come to life, with my Bettie Page bangs and red lipstick. I was easily flattered so I said yes to dinner. We went through three large sakes before I took a trip to the restroom where I dry-swallowed a 5mg Oxy. By the time I said yes to going back to your apartment a thick fog had descended over my brain.

The first thing you did was blindfold me. From there you took off my clothes, bound my wrists and attached me to some set-up you had installed in your doorway. The objects you hit me with and the objects you inserted into my body made me feel like an object myself, something free of a voice and free of thoughts. I assumed that, as a mostly-gay man with an amateur dungeon and so many sex toys, when you inserted yourself you'd include a condom, but later I figured out this wasn't the case. By that point, I couldn't get mad because I hadn't asked.

When you were done with me, I went onto your patio, without speaking to you or dressing first, and smoked a cigarette. You lived on a hill; from your balcony I saw lights and then lights, a band of darkness and then, miles away, the constellation that made up Tijuana. I thought about the people who might be in that band of darkness so late at night, trying to cross undetected from one side to the other.

The air was cool and gave me goosebumps. I blew out smoke and everything inside me was empty and still, as though you'd beaten out the dust. A few weeks later I went to Planned Parenthood, where I was asked if I'd "engaged in any high-risk activity," and I didn't know what to say, not knowing the equations necessary to calculate the severity of risk.

DEAR ETHAN,

I was trying to get clean and I just couldn't figure out how to settle my mind. I'd forgotten a set of house keys at your house the week before while blacked-out, and it occurred to me that you might do the trick when I went to retrieve them. I was wrong. Being naked with you, dead sober, just made every thought ring louder, an inescapable roar coming from the failure of our limbs to find some sort of meaning in the hallway light. I left when you went to use the bathroom because I didn't know how to say goodbye.

The next time I saw you, something had gone wrong. You weren't making sense and didn't have a home and were missing at least three of your teeth. I know from experience that it's difficult to distinguish the consequences of mental illness from those of drugs, so I don't know if it was meth or crack or something less preventable, maybe schizophrenia. By then I'd completed another degree and had nine cavities filled. We are told that that kind of sickness isn't contagious, but I couldn't get it out of my head that I'd infected you.

II

HOW DO I MAKE THE BAD THOUGHTS STOP

Recurring Intrusive Thoughts

Sometimes when I think about myself, I see my body on the beach. Except there is no water. So I guess it's actually a desert. I see my body in the desert, splayed across the sand and the sun is very bright. It is hot. It is so hot that my skin gets soft, a little softer, and then it begins to melt. My nose flops over first, and then my thighs go, and my breasts are dripping down in rivulets, across my ribcage, trickling down my armpits. My organs sludge out too, staining the sand wet, and then all that's left are my bones. I am very skinny.

Sometimes when I'm having a conversation with someone else and it's boring me or I don't like where it's headed, I think about grabbing the other person by the hair and bashing their face into the wall. It doesn't matter where the actual conversation is taking place; in my mind the wall is always made of stucco. It's cream-colored, the kind that is very common in the southwest. Their nose goes in first, and you can see the bone, the depths of their sinus cavities, and then their teeth chip away like lumber. The scalp separates and I am holding the bloody hair in between my fingers, wondering where it all went wrong.

Sometimes when I look at a cute baby or an animal I think about it getting run over by a train and the noise it would make.

Sometimes when I'm trying to fall asleep I think of a giant, ripping the roof from my house like a sardine can and plucking me off into the night. He takes me home and lays me out on a baking sheet and I am too scared to run away. I'm put in the oven and it is very warm in there and it makes me sleepy. I am left in there for a long time. It feels like decades. Eventually I am all dried up and crispy, so the giant takes me out and chops me into a fine powder and lines me into rails and then he snorts me.

Sometimes when I'm going to get crackers or cereal from the cupboard, I feel fear when I open the box and expect the container to be filled with maggots, with flies buzzing out. Sometimes I hold the box to my ear and shake it a little to make sure I don't hear any squirming inside.

Sometimes when I'm on airplanes I think about me dying, because someone put arsenic into my coffee or something. I stop breathing and my skin turns a little blue. My eyes bulge. I am slumped against the window, and there is blood pouring out my nose. It stains the seat.

Sometimes when a friend calls me on the phone and they want emotional support, all I can think about is them in a wheelbarrow with me pushing. I'm running. There's a lot of rocks in the road, and I have to work real hard to keep the wheelbarrow upright, and to not trip. I'm supposed to get them to the hospital because there's sores opening up all over their body, but I'm thinking it just *has* to be too late. I mean, the sores are filled with pus already. So much pus. It keeps splashing in my eye.

Sometimes when I get real angry, it feels like the cells in my brain are popping and I get very hot on the inside. This causes me to take a step out of the anger for a quick second. I become concerned that this is what it feels like to spontaneously combust. Have you seen those pictures before? It's usually a charred chair, next to it a blackened stump. I will look just like that.

Sometimes when I get in the shower I close my eyes and it seems like I'm no longer actually in the shower. I'm in an alley, and there's a bunch of homeless men pissing in my hair.

Sometimes when I think about what it would be like to be pregnant, I imagine that instead of a baby growing inside me it is a very large worm but with teeth and it is chewing out my uterus. Nine months in, I go to give birth and all that comes out is the worm and its teeth and a lot of blood. The doctors still want me to nurse the worm baby, though. They cradle it and put it in a diaper and give it to me to hold and I am trying to say "No no no" but I am so weak from the birth that all I can do is whine a little. They fold my arms so I am forced to hold it and they latch it onto my breast, which it bites off quickly, and then it's so close to what it was seeking the whole time, which is my heart.

But the funny thing is that whenever I think of you, nothing like this appears. When I think of you, I am helpless and small in your arms and you are stroking my hair. I am helpless and small but I feel very safe; with you I enjoy feeling helpless and small. There is a big big moon and stars dotting maps of smiling lions in the sky and you are singing. The melody causes us to drift up and float, higher and higher, and the stars swallow us, swallowing us in a way that will enable us to always be together, to never bleed or rot, or feel anger or pain, or hurt.

Flame War

Everyone is talking about witch hunts
like they're a bad thing
but I think
it could be fun.
If they had some
maybe I could finally know
how other people looked at me.
Like if they thought I was scary.
Because if it were my choice
I would totally burn myself.
Getting tied up on a pole seems sexy
and as I burned
I could pretend
I was offering myself
up to God.

Sexy Terrorist

I want to be a sexy monster
unstoppable and
stomping on everything
destroying until it has
all been crumbled
to rubble and powder bones
with nothing to hear but my
howl

I want to be a sexy terrorist
bombs strapped below my
sexy hips explosions burst
on TV news and when
the cops come I am not
afraid to die because
I believe
in things

I want to be a sexy murderer
the scary person breathing
on your phone the one who
shattered your window
left palm prints on the
bed sheets
and stabbed a knife in your
throat

None of this poem is hyperbole
or inserted in here simply because
the images are evocative
of any particular emotional truth.
I really do want to be a
sexy monster.
sexy terrorist.
sexy murderer.

I want to be terrible, powerful, a
force to be reckoned with, which
means I'm
insane.

Sexy Terrorist Part II

In 2005 my best friend
had a birthday party themed
"Ass, Titties, and Freedom"
so I went dressed as
a sexy terrorist,
which involved a bikini
fake dynamite and
a clock set to 9:11.
I wrote things on my arms like
HELL YEAH AL QAEDA
and
DOWN WITH THE USA
because I was against "freedom"
and found it the opposite
of sexy.
People looked at me
disapproving;
the strangers at the party
would not talk to
me or share
their drugs.
Even my friends said
"Too soon"
– another concept
I disagree with because
there is no such thing.

It is never
too
soon
for anything.

All The Bad News In 2014

(UPDATE: ALSO IN 2015, AND 2016 TOO)

When something bad happens in the collective consciousness
you can hear some real pain
but mostly it is obfuscated by the static
of people saying:
"I care too."
"I am sensitive."
"I promise you I am a good person."

Inner Monologue

WHO CARES WHO CARES WHO CARES
WHO CARES WHO CARES WHO CARES
WHO CARES WHO CARES WHO CARES
WHO CARES WHO CARES WHO CARES
WHO CARES WHO CARES WHO CARES
WHO CARES WHO CARES WHO CARES
WHO CARES WHO CARES WHO CARES
WHO CARES WHO CARES WHO CARES
WHO CARES WHO CARES WHO CARES
WHO CARES WHO CARES WHO CARES
WHO CARES WHO CARES WHO CARES
WHO CARES WHO CARES WHO CARES
WHO CARES WHO CARES WHO CARES
WHO CARES WHO CARES WHO CARES
WHO CARES WHO CARES WHO CARES
WHO CARES WHO CARES WHO CARES
WHO CARES WHO CARES WHO CARES
WHO CARES WHO CARES WHO CARES
WHO CARES WHO CARES WHO CARES
WHO CARES WHO CARES WHO CARES
WHO CARES WHO CARES WHO CARES
WHO CARES WHO CARES WHO CARES
WHO CARES WHO CARES WHO CARES
WHO CARES WHO CARES WHO CARES
WHO CARES WHO CARES WHO CARES
WHO CARES WHO CARES WHO CARES
WHO CARES WHO CARES WHO CARES
WHO CARES WHO CARES WHO CARES

YEAH I DON'T CARE

I Call Bullshit

The thing about drunk driving
is you're not supposed to
talk about how fun it is.

How Should A Person Be

I was concerned about
coming across as a
bad person
in these poems
but my husband said
I shouldn't worry,
that I was
a mean person,
and nasty,
and I just needed to
accept that,
because we are all mean
and nasty underneath
our skin
and anyone who denies this
is a liar.

Win Friends, Influence People

I learned by reading two poetry books
– one from McSweeney's and the other
lauded in The New Yorker –
that my poems make too much sense.
I need to make less sense.
Three blind mice.

They also need more sex
so here
you
go:

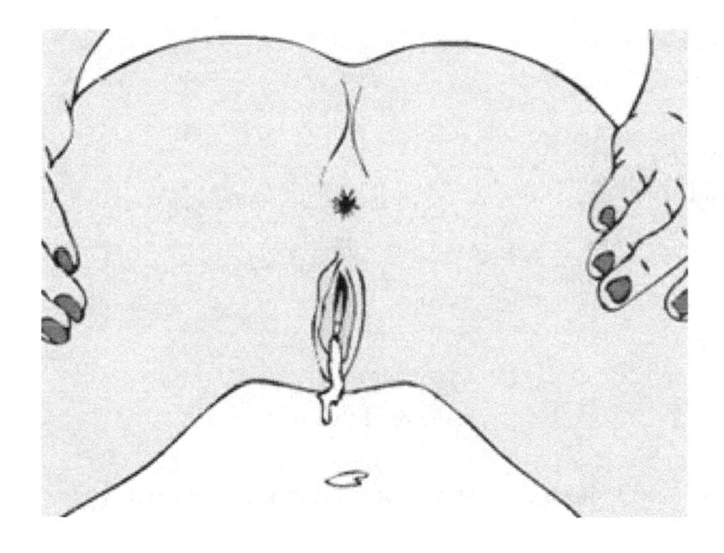

Also I think I might be too pretty.
So it's a good thing I am aging
and gaining weight
because I want the people
to find me
relatable.

I Went To College You Know

I danced
        in the moral error
        of Foucault,
        acolyting into nothing,
        slaking
        and savage.

I bled
        in the situation

        of my

        coteric uterus—
        not even

        Simone
        could save
        me.

I prostituted
        myself

like Sonya,   and my heart was

        empty and I shook the sleeves of God in my daguerreotype.

My father
died
in Nebraska   but Antonia
did not know
                my tutelary.

The impotence
        of Chatterly

meant nothing to me,
he came on me anyway,
his
semen
splashing
on my tendentious toil
turned tricks
before it

sank.

I do not know
any of these
references I have
not read any of these
books
I don't know a lot of
these words
either I just
wanted you
to think I am
smart
did it work

Spite Poem

Remembering the time
when my professor told me
her publicist took advantage
because she was young, attractive, and female.
Except she wasn't that young
or attractive.

III

BIPOLAR NATIONAL ANTHEM

Teen Angst

When I was fifteen I tried to kill myself
by swallowing pills and gin.
At the mental hospital they stabbed
my arms
every morning
five am,
with thick needles, not really caring
if they hit the vein first try, just digging.
Pretty quick the crook of both arms
bruised over and scabbed.
The milk in the lunchroom came in bags
meant to be punctured by straws
and tasted like hormones and glue.
I was in there over Fourth of July.
My roommate was a girl named Charlie,
the best cutter I ever met,
scars on her thighs thick as ropes.
She said it went so deep she nearly bled
to death but that she never
intended to die.
Tiny windows in our room scratched-up
shatterproof glass. Through them
we watched the fireworks from Sea World.

Contemporary Guilt

when i went home
the first time
after going off to get married
my mother begged me: please don't have a baby.

here were her reasons:

1. it would have problems
2. i have problems
3. my husband has problems
4. all the problems would be parts of a real disaster and she wouldn't be able to deal so essentially she'd have to disown me

predictably, i got mad and
stormed off to what used to be my bedroom.

which is the place where
i tried to
kill myself
four times
half a lifetime before.

in the morning, she apologized
– kind of –
asking if i understood what she meant
that she was speaking
out of love
but also fear.
she told me there were things
she never told me
because she had to pretend to be strong.
i think that was when i was supposed to ask
about the things i never knew
but i failed to.

a few days later, i asked her when she knew
that i'd turn out "okay"—
eighteen, twenty-two, twenty-five?
but she was honest
and said it didn't come until i was
living in new york,
two years sober.
that she used to watch the wine bottles pile up
my skin yellow
teeth darken
and that smell.

i guess that's a long time to be
worried
that your daughter is going
to die.

Hanging From The Family Tree

I bake six pies for
Christmas
Clean the house wrap
The presents but later
I am crying
Pulling hair and breaking
Things
Locked alone
In the bedroom with
Him begging me
To open and asking
What is wrong and
My answer –
Nothing.

My father never speaks
Of his dead mother
Because
She used to beat him
When I asked one
Time what
She
Was like he described a
Woman
Who acted just
Like
Me.

Help Desk

somet
imes
it's ha
rd to k
now if
you're
still al
ive so
here i
s a su
refire
way to
tell:

Medical Problems

If one cattle
gets sick
you must kill
the whole lot,
corral them in
a pen and
shoot off
their heads.
It helps
if you play
red queen.

There is only
one way
to prepare my
pneumonic device:
breathing
fresh air until
the letters forget
what it is
they help to
remember
and/or make
sick.

If you blow
into
the stick
the man
inside
the pipe
will smile.
If you do it
hard enough

something else
will happen.
That part is a
surprise.
That part is up
to you.

An allergy test means
pokes
– needles and swabs –
perhaps something else.
When they stick it
inside
your vagina
don't forget
to register
the presence
of blood.

The staples in
my arm
were put there
by a country
doctor he had
to do some numbing
first it came inside me
never forgetting the
smoke clouds
never forgetting
the hour
of my
birth.

I wanted a
loophole
so I made one
out of rope
inside it I put
my head
in the end my
feet dangled the
bracelet
explaining my
condition
dangled off my
toes I dangled
off
the earth.

Say Hello To My Childhood Friend

The monster in my head
is the same size as the big kids
on the back of the bus.
Watch them singing:
murder book,
doom days,
kingdom come.
The apocalypse is not
something I asked
for but it may
be something
I wanted.
That's not what
I can say
about you.

Who Says That Fast Food Can't Bring A Spiritual Awakening

the feeling would be
of summer with the window
open
while on a mild-to-moderate
dose of synthetic opiates
and having forgotten temporarily
that one existed
after vomiting
a small order of
onion rings and
chicken fries
from burger king

Life Is A Joke Sometimes

I went to a new psychiatrist
today. I had to drive an hour
to get there
because the ones
in this town just want
to get you high.
I had to tell her my story.
The whole thing.
The suicide attempts, the drugs,
the hospitalizations,
the relationship I had
as a teen where he left bruises.
At the end, she told me
I was a poster child,
the ideal result of someone
with a story like mine.
Which is funny because
I've never felt like
the poster child
for anything.
Yep. That's me.
The poster child
for mental health.

Top 10 Greatest Feels

10.
Going to work, which means putting
on the same black skirt and
blouse as yesterday, taking your
apron from your locker,
smoking a quick cigarette,
and resigning to the fact that
today is the same as yesterday
and neither likes you
very much.

9.
Sitting on a hospital bed
with the lights out because
you insisted and
the orderlies are afraid
which seems… bad…
because they've probably
seen a little of everything,
so it turns out you're a
unique snowflake
after all.

8.
One of the things about
death
is it just gives you another
justifiable reason
to be angry.

7.
There's at least
five people out there
who genuinely hate you
and there's no way to
apologize because
none want to speak to you,
so maybe that's not that different
from actually having been
absolved.

6.
Four am, nightlight projecting
his shadows on the walls
and the pills have kicked in
but you're still there,
still awake,
feeling the invisible bugs
crawl around on
your skin
which, in some ways,
is a kind of
conjure.

5.
Drowning in a pool of water
that may or may not
actually be there
while listening to 1983's
number one hit record
and not really giving
a shit
either way.

4.
Accepting at age thirty
that you've never been in any
position to take care of
yourself,
that a rose garden
is more
self-sufficient,
so why not let
someone truly love you.

3.
Realizing it's impossible
to differentiate the mistakes
you've made from those
that were merely stupid
decisions,
but fuck wisdom
anyway.

2.
Getting to the point where
hearing that one song
no longer makes you feel
ashamed, and the scent
of coconut rum no longer
reminds you of your own
shoddy attempt
at death.

1.
What's the point of wondering
what the future holds
when the past makes absolutely
zero sense at all.

IV

NATURE POEMS ARE BORING

On The Construction Site Behind My House

If you want to make a road
you have to cut down some trees,
light some bushes on fire.
Watch the rabbits run away,
fleeing their homes and tiny babies.
Yep, that's why it's good
to be human.

Fur Trade

I had a dream the other night where I was a bear.
I had caught myself after
spending several afternoons tracking my scent.
I took a knife and dragged the tip across my bear throat
bleeding a curtain of rich bear blood before
turning the knife to split myself down,
the gentle peeling of my bear belly.
My insides spilled out
in the prettiest shades of purple and red.
I pulled them out slowly,
heavy like jewels in my bear hands.
I gave them to you.
I presented them to you as a necklace.
You put it on and it
looked so lovely against your eyes.

Animals In Winter

My first winter somewhere cold and
animals staying alive seems impossible
because I thought "hibernation" meant
holing up somewhere and going to sleep
for a long while
which, as a human, is just called
giving up.

Turns out it means hearts beating
half as fast and
body temperatures
falling near freezing.
Cold veins, a slow heart—
a means to survive.

The Scenic Route

We were going the back way to the post office
driving through the alley
behind Lowes and the Walmart where
the workers smoked cigarettes in secret.
It had just rained
and everything glistened.

There was this big field, fenced in but
With nothing in it to protect
except for hundreds of crows.
I asked why the birds were there
and he said that's just what crows do:
hang out together in fields.

But then I looked a little closer
and there was this dead dog,
I think the one we'd seen wild
behind our house, the one I wanted
to trap so it didn't freeze that winter.
Anyway, it was dead.

Stomach bloated, legs stiff out,
pointy in rigor mortis.
The crows were eating at it,
making a lot of noise and cackling.
That's the real reason why they were there.
Dog party.

Haiku For Horse Haters #1 – Four-Finger Discount

every time i look
at your teeth i think about
bloody stump fingers

Haiku For Horse Haters #2 - The Joke's On You

if i break my leg
i just go to the doctor.
you do it, you're dead.

Haiku For Horse Haters #3 - Exotic Pets

down in tijuana
people paint you black and white
and call you zebra

Haiku For Horse Haters #4 - Dumb Bitch

shoved nails in your foot
burnt my name onto your rump
now you know you're loved

Haiku For Horse Haters #5 - Real Talk

this isn't a joke
i really do hate horses
they should all just die

How To Talk To Ghosts

1. Turn off the light.

2. Make sure your eyes are

W I D E

O P E N

3. Start to cry.

4. When you ask yourself why you are crying, remember there is

n
o

r
e
a
s
o
n

5. When there is nothing left

6. Open your

M

O

U

T

H

and begin
7. To speak

8. But please remember to say

nothing

of any substance

because
one
must not
frighten

V

RELOCATION

Flight 6256

The baby
is screaming
like I want to
scream
and the man's bald spot
looks so soft
I want to pet it
and I don't see
any time
in between.

There is an amusement park
on the ground with
rollercoasters
like shoestrings
and the hills still
hold green leaves but
when we took off
what lay beneath
was a snowstorm
and coal mills
and a graveyard.
One hour
can change nothing
and so much.

Make A Fist

I always liked the way
it felt
when the needle
slipped in
as they took my blood
except one time
they dug too deep and
it spilled
all over
the linoleum.

My mother
never speaks
about her family;
if you ask,
she just brings
it right back
to me.

When you fly over
the west,
the earth
has cracks you'd
never be able
to see out of
from the ground.

Chemistry Lab

Behind my house is a fence
the other side is bottles
some containing nothing
some containing meth.
Inside plastic the crystals
glow brighter
than what you gave me
including my own bound
wrists.
A science fact:
Blood is redder
after midnight.
Another:
Forgetting has
no atomic weight,
memories
heavier than just about
anything
but the funny thing is
the absence of a
nucleus.

This Poem Was Made Possible By Money And A Few Movements Of My Hand (Which Makes It No Different Than Any Other Poem)

Foxcroft Shell, 619
1000 Foxcroft Avenue
Martinsburg, WV 25401

05/24/2015 3:32:08 PM
Register: 1 Trans #: 5012 Op ID: 1921
Your cashier: Alice

*** PREPAID RECEIPT ***

REGULAR CA PUMP# 2	$25.00	99
SIMPLY LEMONADE W/	$1.99	102
DIET MT DEW	$1.79	101
MARS MILKY WAY S C	$1.29	102
HRSHY TAKE 5	$1.29	102
S JIM GIANT CRACKD	$1.69	102

Subtotal =	$33.05	
Tax =	$0.11	

Total =	$33.16	
Change Due =	$-66.86	
Cash	$100.02	

NEVER PAY FULL PRICE FOR GAS AGAIN!
Join the Shell Fuel Rewards Network
for free and save money on gas when
you purcahse specially marked products.

ROCs Customer Service Hotline
1 (304) 262-5088

I Am The Real Caligirl

Over Christmas my mother
tells me about a license plate
she saw on an Explorer.
The state was Wisconsin
but the message was
CALIGIRL.
The girl was mistaken
because CALIGIRL
is something not to be on
display but hidden in your
heart.

Good News: Gentrification Is Possible Everywhere

In winter I wanted
Adventure so we
Drove through the
Fog to the Old Stone House,
A building that was
Old and dilapidated,
Two qualities he
Thought I'd
Enjoy.
The house was
Registered, an
Official historic site,
Marked with a
Sign at the fork
Off the interstate.
When we arrived
It no longer looked
How he'd remembered it,
Now remodeled, its walls
A sunny stucco,
Bright Christmas lights
Hanging off the
Eaves. In the driveway
Was a Suburu, outfitted
With mountain bikes
And kayaks; you could
Tell the residents were
True people of nature,
Evolved and
Spiritual; you
Could see it in the
Bumper sticker that
Read "Namaste."

Double Exploitation

Chris's girlfriend came over
and told us about her brother
who wrote short stories,
an Iowa grad.

How he exploited
all the things
that had made her
childhood
hers.

The worst was a man named
Rudy who was
mentally disabled
and gay.

Her first boyfriend
gave him a
blow job
so he would buy beer
for the party
where they first hooked up.

In college she
went over to Rudy's house
after his birthday; he'd been out to a
gay bar
the night before –
had bought condoms
expected romance, but left
lonely
and dejected.
He had a pen knife
because he liked to cut

himself
when things were bad,
so she took it away
and calmed him down
but when she left,
she gave it back, so
the cutting reverted to
his decision.

Rudy is probably
dead now
but his exploitation
lives on.
Long live the
exploitation
of marginalized
people.

The Name Of This Poem Is A Picture

We walk around your parents' house and you are
telling me how when you were in high school
you used to
pretend you were on English moors
but all I can see is
West Virginia.

The sky is only light enough
to catch the edge of trees
how they bleed and feather
into mountains.
There are bats.

We walk to the property line
and look at the forest
and it is so dark at first
there is nothing to see
but if you wait
sky pokes in through branches.
Something old waits
trying to push us out
trying to pull us in
it wraps around our wrists and
things are flickering. It is making me feel
a little restless.

And then a dark thing
creeping
screeches at us. It's sudden.
I forget my breath
until I notice its shape
which is the same as me and you.
It is familiar and so
I feel okay again.
We wave at ourselves.
We are calling to ourselves.

VI

TRUE ROMANCE

Long Distance Love Poem

Three things drew me to you
and none of them can I name right now,
but that doesn't mean they don't exist.

Sometimes I sleep until the afternoon
and still won't get out of bed.
My purpose would be to listen
to you breathe, if you were here,
except you're not and so I have none,
but that doesn't mean I'm not conscious of your breaths.

I read the Wikipedia article for nicotine last night.
In small doses, it is a stimulant,
at larger ones, a sedative.
Which is similar to the effect your hand has when it's on my thigh.

Astral Project My Pussy

Sometimes when I am
having sex with
you I like
to pretend that I am no
longer inhabiting my
body.

Not because I don't
enjoy it but
because it seems
counterintuitive
for what we
are trying
to accomplish.

There is no joy
in arms no
intimacy
in knees no
transcendence
in toes
so let us
dissolve
their existence.

Is This What You Wanted

If you promise to
love me, I will
promise to
never act like
myself for
you.

Fairy Tale Before Bedtime

It took me a while to realize
that rain drops were
falling on my
head.
Remember the corpse of
the kitten you buried
in the forest
right after
we met.
I would like to buy its
bones back
encircle them into a
halo
wear it on top of
my head.
Put on bleeding shoes
with silver soles
while holding you.
Pop a bottle of
champagne feed you
cake and call it
a wedding.

That Was Then, This Is Now

The first time we were together on purpose
we walked through the streets of Philadelphia in the rain.
Neither of us lived there and I made a Tom Hanks joke.
You wanted to get a cab but I wouldn't let you,
my reasoning being that a cab costs money
and walking is free. You still drank then,
and your hands were shaking so
we stopped to buy you beer and I waited for you
outside the store, a few feet from a homeless man,
who almost said something to me but thought better of it
when he saw the look in my eye,
something in it more unhinged
than him.
We went back to the hotel and ordered pizza
we never ate because
neither of us were healthy enough to have appetites.
I wouldn't let you touch me but
that would change in a couple months,
because by then I no longer smelled
the scent of death in your footsteps.

Handle With Care

When you tie me up
please be sure to break
my body as I
am no longer
any good
at breaking it
myself.

Please feel free
to remove
my skin,
peel me like
a vegetable,
make me smaller,
into a desirable
shape and eat
me because
I want to be
bite-sized.

When we go to bed
do not forget
to set fire to
my hair;
this is the only hope
I have for
being smarter
in the morning.

If you feel the
need to forget
me in the car on a
hot day, there is
no need to lower

the window my blood
needs a good boiling
anyway.

Fight Poem #1 - Ample Apology

Sorry for kicking you in the stomach.
I didn't know you were in there
until you were
balled up in the corner of the bathroom
and screaming.
I swear it won't happen again.

Fight Poem #2 - Bedtime Story

The Dateline last night was about a preacher
who killed
each of his wives.
I can't see a bit of that inside you.
Although there was that time I woke up from bad dreams
begging for a promise
that you wouldn't murder me.
That was weird.
Maybe I meant to say it to myself
about myself.
That seems a lot more likely.

Fight Poem #3 – No Coffeemaker

We got into it because
he wouldn't get the coffee
and he knows how I am
in the mornings

from the Seroquel.

A point well understood
until his doctor put him
on the same medicine.
But he doesn't need a bra
for the hotel lobby.

His refusal seemed absurd, like
inconveniencing me on purpose,
so I picked up his backpack and
removed the contents, dropping
each item individually on the floor.

At the time
it felt biblical
– an eye for an eye –
but looking back, I admit
it was a dick maneuver.

Fight Poem #4 - Where's That Mirro

He kept on asking me
if I was OK, implying his awareness
of my emotional states
was greater than my own.
And maybe it is.
Maybe I still
do not know myself.

Fight Poem #5 - Broken Promise

I told my husband it
was time for working,
not kissing.
He said if I
didn't kiss him
he would jump
out the window.
I didn't kiss him but
he didn't
jump.

Fight Poem #6 – Dramatic Recreation

Most of our arguments are over
something stupid and
this one was
no exception.
In this one, I was
the bad guy, the
one who had
a temper tantrum for
no reason.

Later, that night
before bed, I had you
recreate my actions
from earlier, which involved
foot stamping, spinning in
circles, hands over ears,
and exaggerated cries.
Damn.
I looked cool.

True Romance

I.
I'll let you fuck me
if you make it quick.
Like mechanized.
Like we both come
and that's it.
No funny business
in between.

II.
Now that irony
has been milked to death,
what is left?
You wearing a fake beard
while riding me?
I'd like to bear
your weight, carry you
until I collapse,
carry you
until I die.

III.
It's funny that the
first time I
kissed you,
you were a fat
sad drunk,
suicidal with your skin
sweaty and red.
I must have been
real desperate
or in love.

IV.
The one time
during sex when
you told me
you wanted a
Subway sandwich
without realizing
how it sounded.

V.
When I went back
to California you
caught the flu and shit
all over the bathroom
and in the tub.
I made you bleach everything
before I would go in there
but a couple days later
I was taking a bath
and I saw
what might have been
a speck of shit
on the side of the tub.
I didn't wipe
it away.
Instead I bathed
in it.
I'm still bathing in it.
I will always be bathing
in your feces.

VI.
Unseasonably hot
the day

of our wedding,
so you padded your suit
with paper towels in hopes
of soaking up
the sweat.
It didn't work.
Dancing with you
made my cheek wet.

VII.
I held up my hair
off my neck and asked
you to describe to me
the pimple that
was growing there.
It is huge and nasty,
bright red, you said.
It looks like a boil.
It looks like something
died there.
But then you kissed it.

VIII.
We showed up early
to the birthday dinner
so I told you to park next
to the dumpster
and made you jerk off
in front of me to kill
time.
I giggled at you,
the faces you made,
but yeah, I was a little
aroused.

IX.
The one time I picked
my nose
and you ate
my booger.
The time I sent you
fingernail clippings
in the mail.
When we cut our palms
with straight razors
and blended together
our blood.
I am inside you.
You have become
my home.

X.
There are ten sections
in this poem
because you are
obsessed with the
number ten.
Whoever said
I wasn't a
romantic.

10 10 10 10 10
10 10 10 10 10 10 10 10 10
10 10 10 10 10 10
10 10 10 10 10 10
10 10 10 10 10 10
10 10 10 10 10 10
10 10 10 10 10 10
10 10 10 10 10 10
10 10 10 10 10 10
10 10 10 10 10 10 10 10
10 10 10 10 10 10 10 10

VII

FEAR AND SELF-LOATHING IN VARIOUS STATES

Hot New Diet Tip

This man is saying that the reason
we weigh less in the morning
is because of our breaths
– that they weigh something –
atoms of carbon and water vapor.
But what about the weight of thoughts.
In the mornings, I have so few.
Maybe, in time, I can grow stupider,
grow thinner,
weigh less.

Paragard

It's a piece of plastic
wrapped in wire
that takes up the entire span
of my uterus,
which, when I first saw the
illustrations online,
I thought was an exaggeration.
The giant T, slicing across my womb.

To get it inside:
multiple stick-like
objects inserted into
my hole,
along with two of the doctor's
fingers,
each sending
a separate wave of pain
that made the neon lights
on the ceiling grow dim.
My friend in California said
her doctor gave an anesthetic,
a luxury not offered
in West Virginia –
the burdens of being a hillbilly's
wife.

The IUD will stay for ten years,
a length of time I cannot fathom
because the person I occupied
a decade ago
is someone I do not know,
someone I cannot understand,
someone who now makes me
sick.

Science Experiment

has anyone ever
tried bloodletting
as a remedy
for psychological
maladies

if you need a
volunteer i wouldn't
mind giving it
a go

i mean, i've got
a knife
in my hand
already
so it wouldn't be
that big of a
deal

All I'm Asking For Is Perfection

Everything on you is oily, and everything on you smells bad. The acne is spreading. There is always something that needs covering up. There are always pimples to pop, impurities to expel, and there is only so much the creams can do. The doctor writes you a prescription and forbids you from sunlight. The directions on the tube say APPLY TO AFFECTED AREA but it seems impractical to cover your entire body. Maybe it would be better to eat it. That way you could fix things from the inside.

In the shower, you use the razors that advertise the closest shave. You use special shaving cream that promises the same thing. Afterward you still feel the hairs under your skin so you shave over and over and it is still not completely smooth so you do it harder. You know the hair will begin to grow back immediately anyway. You know it will be spiky again in the morning. Once you're out of the shower, your legs are red and raw and some of the follicles are bleeding. You rub lotion into them and it feels like you're standing in flames.

Long nails are preferable and so you grow yours out. You apply many different ointments to help them along. They're always manicured. The long nails and the polish make your long fingers look even longer. People comment in a way that sounds complimentary but you're not sure; most use words like "graceful" but someone else says "spindly." You discover that it is hard to keep nails this long clean. Everything wants to hide under them: crumbs of food, cosmetics, snot. In traffic, you get into the habit of using one fingernail to clean out another, and what you remove is always pasty and and grey. At work you watch them fly over the keyboard. They look venomous and sharp, like spiders. In the morning, there are scratches on your cheek, three of them, and it is like the devil has been inside your room.

When you were little, you and your father drove out to the high desert. There were wide expanses filled with white pointy windmills, incomprehensibly tall and spinning. Your father said the windmills were good, that this was the cleanest way for us to get power, and he was a person who knew about such things so you knew it was true. The windmills didn't look like good things, though. The blades looked sharp and in them you saw three versions of yourself, each stabbed with a windmill blade in the back, spinning around, too high for anyone to reach, too high to be saved.

There's Blood On My Shoulder

Dear Liza, dear Liza.
So fix the hole.

Q. With what shall I fix it?
A. Someone else's hole.

Baptism

In the bath I watch
my body float and
I am
unable to distinguish
stretch marks from
razor scars.
My right breast is
definitely bigger
and uglier
than the left
though.
My feelings for the
fat
on my stomach
waver;
the lumps are
a good meter for the
type of man you've
snared:
if he compliments,
or ignores.
I married the
kind of man
who kisses it
which should make
me feel beloved
but instead I just
feel obeast,
a fat fuck.

2013 Poem From A 1992 Story

All her friends and family commented on how talented Annie was. But she didn't beleve them.

so she painted a palace with worry after dinner
and purposly chose her ugliest dolls.
her grandparents smelled and in a few hours
Annie was able to focus again.
In front of her home, in the morning light
She watched her Mom struggle
to make something magic,
chaining the worry to windows.
But There was no magic
There was no magic
There was no magic
There were Only walls.

An Instance Of Reverse Psychology

J-Woww's fiancé calls their new daughter "Angel Baby" and means it,
When she goes to get vaccinated he cannot stand to see her cry
Because angel babies come down from heaven.

When I was a teenager my mother took to calling me angel child
My father and even her best friend got in on the act
Years later she told me she thought if she
Said it enough
That maybe I would act like it
Instead of the poco diablito, which is what they
Jokingly
Called me when I was a kid
When I obeyed and got excellent grades.

What Mother Used To Say

My hands are cold and my
heart is an
asshole

It's What's On The Inside That Counts

I would like it if I didn't see my acne
as a manifestation of my inner self
but this is difficult when my thoughts resemble swine
and there is nothing in my heart worth admiration.

I have picked my face until I bled
and cried later over the scabs,
frustrated at my inability to remove myself
from myself.

He says my preoccupation is one of pretty people,
someone with the luxury to focus on spots,
but I see it as something fitting to plague
a woman incapable of unshackling
her adolescence.

True Story

The most honest act I can do
is pop a pimple and watch
the pus squirt onto the
mirror.
Everything else is
dishonest,
deceitful,
a cover-up.

VIII
ANXIETY ATTACKS

January 3, 1999: Portland, OR

I pocketed a box of Coricidin at the drugstore the night before I was set to go back. In the morning I swallow half the box with a glass of orange juice and finish packing my suitcase. Soon it is time to go. My scalp is tingling a little bit but mostly I don't feel anything yet. My mom cries some when she drops me off, but it doesn't really bother me that I have to go, and I wonder briefly if this makes me a bad person.

The plane is about to board and now I feel a little dizzy but that's about it. Maybe you're supposed to take the whole box, I think. I swallow the rest of the pills with warm water from the drinking fountain and get on the plane.

When it comes time to transfer flights in Portland, I stand up and it is like astronaut boots on my feet. I walk through the tunnel from the plane into the airport in what at least feels like a straight line. A cigarette seems like the kind of thing that will make me alright but it's not like I'm exactly thinking clearly. I am rushing past the security check point and maybe I hit someone with my backpack because there's this guy and he's glaring at me. He says something or maybe he yells it but I can't quite make out his words. I get outside and light a cigarette. I smoke so fast the end turns long and skinny like a pencil. I focus everything I have onto that red tip and for the five minutes it lasts I feel OK.

I make it back through security and to my gate without too much trouble. The plane is delayed. I am sitting there listening to my headphones, telling myself everything is fine, I will get on the plane soon, but suddenly my head is so thick I can't breathe. Maybe I am ODing. When my fingers go numb I make myself get up and go into the bathroom. I splash water on my face. I don't dry it off. I lock myself in the handicapped stall, sitting on the toilet, head between my knees, trying to catch my breath. When everything has mostly stopped, I notice that the ends of my hair are wet from something, wet from something that is on the floor of the bathroom. It might be piss.

When I leave the bathroom, my pulse is still jumpy but I'm mostly OK. The plane has all boarded. I make it on just in time. When Wade, the afternoon counselor, picks me up in the white van he doesn't seem to notice anything, and my drug test comes back clean, but I feel dizzy and doomed for two more days.

July 23, 2001: San Diego, CA

I took acid a week ago and I probably shouldn't have. Ever since, and things have been sliding around. Shadows vibrate and phones ring and there's no shadows or phones actually there.

I am smoking cigarettes at the tables at the strip mall where we all hang out. Some people are playing cards. I am not playing cards. I am sitting there, doing nothing, just smoking. People are saying things, joking, talking with each other. I have nothing to say. I try to come up with something but everything in my brain is just noise.

My breaths get short and I know I have to get out of there, tripping over the heavy metal chair as I stand up. I walk quickly until I am out of sight, and then I run. I go behind the movie theater, where there is a stucco wall fencing in the theater's emergency exits. I lay down on the cement. It is cold. I take deep breaths and look at the sky. The sky is warm. I have a Sharpie in my pocketbook and I pull it out. I am lying on the cement. I write on it: CEMENT. My head is next to the stairs. I write on them: STAIRS. My legs are next to a wall. I write on it: WALL. I know where I am in relation to other things. I feel them solid under the tip of the pen.

For the next few weeks, when I feel like things are crowding in, I take out my Sharpie and label what's around me. Soon everything at the strip mall has my handwriting on it.

PLANTER
SIDEWALK
CURB
CHAIR
TABLE
ASHTRAY
BATHROOM

The other kids look at me funny when I do this. They already think

I am weird and this is just a reinforcing act, but I don't seem to have much of a choice. Maybe they think I'm the charming kind of weird. If that doesn't work—well, at least I have a pretty face.

March 9, 2006: Encinitas, CA

He told me he would stop giving me pills when my eyes started watering when I woke up. He said this was a sure sign of addiction. My eyes have been watering for a month at least but he hasn't noticed, or if he has he hasn't said anything yet.

He lives in the garage at his mother's house. It is a separate building and soundproofed, so even though it's at his mother's house there is more privacy than at my apartment, so most nights we sleep here. It is always dark when we wake up because there are no windows, and I look at this as something positive.

We have to go into his mother's house to get coffee. Because of this, I have to wait for him to get up. Last night I couldn't sleep and I'm especially tired. He takes a long time to get fully awake. He, like me, always does it slow. He's the kind of person who you shouldn't talk to in the mornings until he's good and ready. I forget this today, and soon we are arguing.

"Look at your eyes!" he screams at me. "Watering like a fucking junky."

I don't think about the fact that if I am a junky, then he is *really* a junky. I don't think anything logical like that. Instead, something in me snaps, and I am throwing things, CD cases and the wine bottles from the night before, and the wine bottles from the night before that, and they are all exploding against the wall, pop pop pop. He grabs my shoulder to get me to stop. He doesn't mean to be rough, but his fingers are rough anyway because of how I am moving. His fingers feel the way they used to with the boyfriend who was two boyfriends before him, the one I had to get a restraining order against, and the strength behind the fingertips splinters something and suddenly I am on my back nearly choking, and everything is evil, and I am dying, and I can't feel my legs or my arms.

"Breathe," he says, and strokes my hair. I want to swat him away but I can't. He puts a Xanax between my fingertips and I take it to my mouth and chew it up and soon everything slows down enough for me to see straight again.

April 24, 2012: Brooklyn, NY

I don't really know how it happens but we are fighting in our bedroom and the mirror from the wall ended up on our bed somehow? And then it broke and shards and pieces got all over the sheets, and we were wrestling in it, wrestling for the bracelet she had given him but also for control and neither one of us could find any. It ends with him on top of me because he is bigger and stronger. We are breathing hard, our hearts pounding, and the slivers of glass dig into our skin. His face is in front of mine, his big hands on my shoulders, and I hate it that he has won. So I spit in his face.

Later, I see that me spitting is the demarcating line between what was before and the end of our relationship. But at the time it didn't seem like that big of a deal.

He gets off me, and is going out the door, and I am chasing him, but his lead is too much and I am not wearing shoes, and I have no idea where he went. Probably to one of the bars a few blocks away, but my hair is a mess and I can still feel glass in me and I am too ashamed to be in public and searching for him like a jilted woman. So I go back home.

Except besides not having shoes, I also don't have keys or a cell phone and I can't get back into the apartment. I sit on the stoop and although it's a warm night it is still April and it is cold and my feet are cold and I realize that my life with him is going to end now, that one of us will have to move out, that it will probably be me, that he won't be in my life anymore, that I am alone, that I am ugly, that we just yelled and broke things and wrestled in shattered glass on our bed, that I spat in his face, and my feet are cold, and it is cold, and I am locked out, and the world is spinning, and I am worried I am dying and the edges of things grow dizzy and black.

But then a raccoon is crawling up the fence. There is no wilderness anywhere near us, and I've never seen wildlife around here before, and seeing this raccoon here feels like something meaningful. It is perched at the top, looking at me, deciding if I am a threat, weighing its choices. We regard each other for a while. Then it hops my side of the fence and walks slowly down the street, in the direction of where the person who is now my ex-boyfriend has gone, and I can breathe, and things are terrible and ugly and I am still ashamed but I also know things will be OK without him.

October 26, 2014: Somewhere in Ohio

The night before we did a reading in Indianapolis, and now we are driving back home. I haven't been around people that much lately and we stayed up late and I woke up feeling headachey and dehydrated and anxious, the way I did back when I still drank and was hungover. When we stop at a gas station, I buy a pack of cigarettes to complete the feeling, even though I have supposedly quit.

There is so much roadkill this time of year. Some places on the pavement, it is hard to tell if it is paint that has been spilled or blood.

Somewhere in Indiana and we see this deer walking in some grass on the side of the interstate. Its hindquarters look like they have exploded but it is still upright. Neither of us can tell whether it has been shot or run over.

A few weeks ago, I found a picture of a deer with its stomach slit in a magazine and I cut it out and put it above my desk. Now I feel guilty, guilty for conjuring this animal on the side of the road, this thing that is still alive but suffering, this thing that will almost certainly die soon. Its pain and its blood are because of me.

We get into an argument over CDs. It isn't quite as stupid as it sounds; it has something to do with ex-boyfriends. I end up throwing the CDs and they spill all over the car. He yells at me. I pull the hood of my sweatshirt down as far as it goes, and it covers my eyes and I feel protected from the bright light of the sun and also his anger.

But not really. Soon I am crying. Soon I am crying and I can't stop. I try to think about why I am crying but there is nothing. There is nothing wrong except for everything. I am crying so hard I can't catch my breath. I feel like something has gotten me, grabbed hold of me, is making me crazy, a demon or alien clasping onto my brain. And then I am certain my mom has died, certain something terrible has happened to her, and I am crying because my mom is dead.

Eventually we pass from Ohio back into West Virginia. He pulls over at a gas station. The parking lot looks into a McDonald's. All the lights are on, even though it isn't dark yet, and everything seems to be made out of either plastic or glass. The horizon keeps tilting in the neon light. He tells me everything is OK, and I try to believe him. I stop crying. I check the mirror and there are mascara tears on my face, and I clean myself up.

Eventually I am well enough to go inside. I use the restroom and he buys me a Gatorade. I feel embarrassed because there are a lot of people at the gas station and my eyes are all red.

INTERLUDE

The Triangle Shirtwaist Fire Of 1911

The sky that day was blue, so extreme in its clarity that it has a technical term: "Severe clear." A rhyme for unlimited visibility—everything, crystal blue clear, in every direction.

This is what the survivors say. The sky was so blue. It was so beautiful.

New York is perfect in September, the trees still with their leaves and the sunlight thin yellow, the air no longer heavy with the hot garbage smell of the summer. And the beauty of that day was remarkable. A perfect day, a perfect so perfect it hurt.

...

My 9/11 story is so boring. I slept through it. I was high school age but not in high school, working at a chain bookstore. On 9/12/01, people lined up outside the bookstore before we opened. The newspapers sold out immediately. I should have bought one but I didn't. The late edition of the *New York Times* from 9/11/01 is currently for sale on eBay, $1999.99 or best offer.

My drummer ex-boyfriend's story is better. He had just started college, newly arrived in the big city from a small town. Classes were cancelled for weeks. He wandered the city aimlessly, feeling lonely and alone, drinking and smoking on strangers' rooftops, staring at the newly-crafted skyline. A few days later, he had his first and only gay sexual encounter, with a model on one of those rooftops.

...

On 8/15/22, I watch footage of the old film, now remastered in crisp digital. When the jets hit, some of the people scream HOLY SHIT. Some of the people scream OH MY GOD. Some of the people just scream.

As a species, these are the default responses to something that is difficult to comprehend as anything other than terrible. We are programmed machines with three buttons. Six, if you count HOLY

FUCKING SHIT, OH MY LORD, and OH MY FUCKING GOD as separate options.

In the video, I watch the people wearing their private faces—faces normally hidden in bedrooms, restrooms, cubicles, apartments, tucked into chests. Now the private faces are public, looking up, up, up at the sky. Shock and awe and horror and sadness. Disbelief. The private faces, now historical record, shown and reshown to millions of people across the country, across the world. To be shown to me, twenty years in the future. I rewind ten seconds. Is that man crying. I rewind ten seconds. Both men are crying.

...

George W. Bush is sitting in an elementary school, a class of cute kids in cute uniforms sitting in front of him. George W. Bush is listening to one of the children read a story called *The Pet Goat.* There is a sign behind George W. Bush's head that says READING MAKES A COUNTRY GREAT. George W. Bush's Chief of Staff comes up and whispers in his ear. George W. Bush looks around stupidly. He purses his lips. George W. Bush did just about everything wrong but I do agree with his decision to wait for the story to end.

...

If you learn enough about 9/11, you will notice that just about everybody who was there that day was named Mark. The man trapped under the rubble, his name is Mark. The police officer is named Mark. The ambulance driver. Both the lawyer and the newspaper reporter who were staying at the Marriot are named Mark. George W. Bush's Chief of Staff? Mark.

In a video, a man is talking on the phone, walking the streets shortly after the North Tower was hit:

Strong New York accent:

"Yeah, somebody crashed a fuckin' airplane into the fuckin' building.

Yeah, I'm OK. I'm with Mark. Yeah, OK, I love you too. Bye."

Same man, yelling now:

"Mark, over here. Mark, where are you going? Mark, we gotta get outta here. Mark, we're gonna get killed. MARK! MARK! WHERE ARE YOU GOING?"

Coincidentally, four of the men who were responsible for overpowering the hijackers on Flight 93, causing it to crash into a field in Shanksville, PA instead of the U.S. Capitol, were named Mark.

Biblical scholars believe that the Gospel of Mark is the oldest gospel, written around 70 A.D. More than any other gospel, the Gospel of Mark portrays Jesus as a magician.

...

If you want to be an acclaimed literary novelist, you must, at some point, write a 9/11 novel, or, at least, insert it into one of your books. If you don't know where to put it, just put it at the end.

...

In 2018, I am in a small town in Virginia, population 300, on vacation. My husband and I walk to the historic courthouse. We look at the old brick steps. Off to the side, there is an evergreen with a marble plaque below it. It bears two (2) American flags and these words in all caps: DEDICATED TO THE FALLEN VICTIMS VOLUNTEERS AND SURVIVORS OF SEPTEMBER 11 2001.

It feels so oddly specific, here, in rural Virginia.

We keep walking. There are more evergreen trees and more marble plaques with American flags on them. Each is dedicated to a different group of people:

DEDICATED TO THE FALLEN VICTIMS VOLUNTEERS AND SURVIVORS OF PEARL HARBOR

DEDICATED TO THE FALLEN VICTIMS VOLUNTEERS AND SURVIVORS OF THE TRIANGLE SHIRTWAIST FIRE

DEDICATED TO THE FALLEN VICTIMS VOLUNTEERS AND SURVIVORS OF THE SAN FRANCISCO EARTHQUAKE OF 1906
DEDICATED TO THE FALLEN VICTIMS VOLUNTEERS AND SURVIVORS OF THE BUFFALO SUPERMARKET SHOOTING
DEDICATED TO THE FALLEN VICTIMS VOLUNTEERS AND SURVIVORS OF THE AIDS CRISIS
Never forget!

In 2025, I am living in a small town in West Virginia, population 16,000. I receive a postcard in the mail advertising a Christian rally that will be at the convention center down the street. It shows a picture of the New York skyline with two heavenly rays of light shining from the memorial. Except the skyline is wrong. The Empire State building is right next to the memorial and the Chrysler building is missing. The postcard says GOD BLESS AMERICA and 9/11 WE REMEMBER.

I go online and look at the schedule but the details are vague and it seems like it isn't really meant for remembering 9/11 so I don't go.

The next month, they have a rally to remember the San Francisco Earthquake of 1906 and I go to that one and get saved.

But I'm lying. I do, in fact, know the difference between 9/11 and the San Francisco earthquake of 1906. It's optics. There's a reason why people care more about the World Trade Center deaths than those at the Pentagon. It's a lot more fun to watch a skyscraper burn than an office park.

I go to the Walmart in my small town in West Virginia. I see a minivan with a license plate that has a picture of the World Trade Center on it. It says 911 NEVER FORGET.

...

I buy a shirt on eBay that has a photo of Osama bin Laden on it and a photo of George W. Bush and a photo of an American flag. I wear it to bed.

...

In 2015, I'm in Brooklyn, reading poems to an audience, at a building with a view of the new memorial. I read the poem about dressing up as a sexy terrorist for a costume party: fake dynamite, silver bikini, Sharpie on my arms saying "I LOVE AL QAEDA." Nobody at the reading is offended.

...

The photo from the hotel chain where they tell you they are commemorating 9/11 by offering free mini muffins for half an hour in the lobby.

...

On the eleventh anniversary, I post a meme to my Facebook page. It is a fake Subway sandwich ad with a man holding his arms like he is an airplane, pretending to crash into two sandwiches. TWO SUBS $9.11 YOU'LL "NEVER FORGET" THIS DEAL, it reads.

A good friend of a good friend gets mad. He is a vet. He yells at me, via Facebook comments, flame war style. 9/11 IS NOT SOMETHING TO JOKE ABOUT PEOPLE LITERALLY GAVE THEIR LIVES FOR THIS.

A year later, the vet messages me. He wants to talk. We are both in a twelve-step program and he wants to make amends. I tell him this isn't necessary but eventually I agree to meet him for coffee anyway. It is fun. I enjoy the attention and care it takes for somebody to apologize to you for something they did in the past. That is one of the most loving and least pleasant things the twelve step program makes you do: confront your past, not just on your own, but with the people with whom you lived it. You look at what you did wrong and you apologize. There is also something called "a living amends," where you actively decide to quit being shitty to someone you were especially shitty to. My living amends are to my mother and father.

Is that wrong? Should I have volunteered to make amends to him instead?

With 9/11, who owes whom the amends?

...

LET THE BODIES HIT THE FLOOR LET THE BODIES HIT THE FLOOR LET THE BODIES HIT THE FLOOR

– *Drowning Pool (nu metal band), May 2001*

According to Drowning Pool's Wikipedia page: During 2001, the song "Bodies" became popular, but the song was taken off radio stations after the September 11 attacks because it was considered inappropriate in the wake of the terrorist attack. An early version of "Bodies" appeared in their EP *Pieces of Nothing* (2000), featuring a significantly greater amount of screaming.

...

If 9/11 was one of your family members, it would be your sloppy uncle at Thanksgiving, when he gets too drunk and sentimental and starts flinging his arms, accusing people of slighting him, and then he tries to start a fistfight but accidentally starts crying instead.

If 9/11 was a sandwich, it would be a McRib.

If 9/11 was a natural disaster, it would be a forest fire.

If 9/11 was a small household appliance, it would be an air fryer.

If 9/11 was a zodiac sign, it would be a Leo.

If 9/11 was a dog, it would be a golden retriever.

If 9/11 was a health insurance company, it would be COBRA.

If 9/11 was a country, it would be America.

The most American part of America, 9/11, our jingoism and bravery and our tacky pride. Our big shiny buildings and our loud bombs and our prayers. Our tragedy.

...

A man, calmly eating a sandwich downtown, the North Tower burning in the background. The second jet hits. The man recoils in horror, runs away. What happened to the sandwich?

...

I talk about 9/11 so often that my husband says I must call it something else. He can no longer tolerate me saying the phrase "nine eleven." His preference is that I stop mentioning it, period, but if I can't do that, I should refer to it as "the tragedy" instead.

When I ask him to read this story, he says it is good but there are too many "9/11's." I should cut some. I listen to him and cut nine of them, but then add one (1) more.

...

A man in Miami owned a taipan snake (super venomous) as a pet. Bad idea! The snake bit him on 9/11/01. Hospitals don't carry non-regional anti-venom. It has to be flown in. But on that day, all the planes were grounded. Bad luck! He started bleeding out of his eyes and mouth. Finally they made an exception for him, flew in a plane with the anti-venom from a special facility in San Diego, escorted by two fighter jets. Imagine the medical bill! He lived.

The same day, a famous American herpetologist was conducting research in Myanmar. He got bit by a snake. There were communication problems with the embassy and the weather was bad and he didn't get the anti-venom in time. He died.

...

The jet fuel ignited as it spilled down the elevator shafts, blowing out the whole lobby and the only in-tact stairwell.

...

There were women's shoes everywhere, at Ground Zero and the Pentagon. All the living ladies and all the dead ladies, bodies blown out of dress shoes.

...

Hi. I'm on the 100th floor of the World Trade Center with thirty people. It's hard to talk. There's a lot of smoke. We're all overreacting. Please come right now. Okay, bye.

...

The priest at Ground Zero saw an ambulance so he went to give the people inside it their last rites. But there were no dying people in the ambulance. Instead, it was filled with dogs, dogs wearing oxygen masks, dogs struggling to breathe, dogs dying. They died from sniffing in the rubble.

The woman who worked in the morgue waited for the bodies to arrive, but no bodies came. It was pieces of bodies that showed up instead. A body bag, an arm. A body bag, a chunk of a torso. A body bag, a thigh.

She says the ones still wearing clothes were most useful because sometimes there were things in their pockets. Coins, slips of paper, items more identifiable than limbs and organs. Our selfhood is not contained in our flesh, but in our trash. The body bags were so light and easy to carry, like those of a baby.

The people who worked in the hospitals waited for the injured people to arrive, for the chaos, but no people came. The hospital was peaceful. There were no patients because the people were all dead.

...

Things that fuse together in extreme heat: contact lenses to eyeballs, fabric to flesh.

Things that tear apart in extreme heat: fire retardant coating, steel.

...

As the World Trade Center burned, a fireman had to leave to change his uniform. He was standing too close to one of the falling bodies and got a chunk of human remains stuck to his pants.

...

The line cook's shift begins at 8 a.m. First thing, prepping the walk-in cooler. Walk-in coolers have a thick seal and thick walls, rendering them soundproof. The line cook is in the cooler for about fifteen minutes. When he comes back outside, nobody is around. They've disappeared. A customer walks into the kitchen. "You can't be in here," the line cook tells him.

It is then that he notices a crazed look in the customer's eye. A streak of fear shoots through him.

The customer says, "No, but COME AND SEE."

The line cook tries to leave the kitchen with the customer, but something is blocking the door. Some kind of dead animal. The line cook is confused. What is a dead animal doing here, in this restaurant, in the kitchen? But then he notices it is not a dead animal. It is a dismembered arm.

He tries to go back to safety, back to the walk-in cooler.

But again, the customer says, "No, but COME AND SEE."

Twenty years in the future, the line cook tells the documentary camera: "AND I SAW."

He beheld the courtyard.

In it there are hundreds of bodies, but just the parts. Dismembered arms and legs and heads. And right then, a body comes and falls in front of him, hitting the ground, BOOM. It explodes into pieces.

...

But I love the businessman who saved the burning woman and the off-duty priests and nurses and Port Authority employees who fled their homes to help and I love the group of men who carried their friend who had no legs to safety. I love the crew of firefighters who saved Josephine Harris, a woman who could barely walk due to a recent car accident. And I love that in the end, it was she who saved them: if they weren't slowed by saving her, they would have been elsewhere in the building and it would have collapsed on them and they would be dead. I love the people rescuing the crowds with their boats, I love the firefighters, I love the police officers, I love the everyday small acts of kindness, the woman who shared her asthma inhaler and the woman who got the man a bottle of water and the bodegas giving out free sandwiches and the man who literally gave a woman the shirt off his back. I love the EMT partners, separated by chaos, only to find each other and reunite in the rubble. I love the stories of people praying together. I love the two men who saved each other, agreeing to be brothers for life, rubbing their bloody palms together in oath. Each and every one of them, small, living angels, carrying out a moment of grace. Come and see this too.

...

Found at the crash site of United Flight 93: a snake, coiled up, ready to strike, preserved in ash like Pompei; an entire face, separated from the skull, most likely belonging to one of the hijackers; a chunk of skin bearing a Superman tattoo, from the body of Louis "Joey" Nacke II, most likely one of the passengers who wrestled control of the airplane from the hijackers; a Bible, nearly pristine, its still-white pages fluttering in the wind, before falling open to Mark 9:

Their worm does not die
And the fire is not quenched.
Their worm does not die
And the fire is not quenched.
Their worm does not die
And the fire is not quenched.

God Poem IV

In the notebooks I kept
As a teenage miscreant
I dislodged a ghost

It was accidental but
Now I sleep with
A knife

God Poem III

If you want to speak to God
I recommend yelling
but follow up with a
self-deprecating joke,
something about the
way you were brought up,
maybe the shape of your nose.

I heard he likes altars,
ones built from capitalism,
disposable plastic products –
tampon applicators,
old calculators,
grocery bags –
that kind of thing.
For glue, use mucus.
Any hole will do.

Generally babies
don't matter but if He
decides He wants one,
make sure it is
extra pink,
has all its fingers.

God Poem II

Under water I can
hear the world strum
as it holds us barely
tethered, sucked into
the drain.
If I open my eyes
I am reminded of
my first time in the
ocean,
ozone thinner in the
wrong hemisphere, sting of
sun,
buried murk waves,
foot white and
my father whispering
"there's sharks."

God Poem I

If God is so great
then why did He make bodies
with so many flaws
so many ways to twist or
disintegrate
Just like a man, I
tell you

How To Upset A Californian

In quarantine, you can't
recycle so I throw
the cans in the
trash.

Ha! Fuck you, earth!

Self-Knowledge Is The Key To Something

I have learned a new thing
about myself:
I love digging
in the dirt.

Things My Students Have Emailed Me In The Past Couple Weeks

I am sorry but my essay is bad, my son dumped the kitty litter box into the air conditioning vent, poop and all.

I am sorry but I can't do the homework tonight, my aunt killed herself.

I am sorry that I've been slacking off, my boss is making me drive to Indiana, I am sleeping in my truck because I am too scared of the disease to stay in a hotel.

I am sorry but last night a tree fell on my house, I am lucky to be alive.

I am sorry but I need an extra day, I can't stop crying or feeling homicidal there is no in between.

Another Nature Poem

Here, in the springtime,
the birds are so loud,
like all they want
is to kill each other.
The only comparison I can find
in humans:
        -The internet
        -Wrestling matches
Maybe we are
appropriating the birds'
culture. We should stop.
Leave it to the birds.

Next comes summer.
Flood rains, hail storms,
the woods chock
full of deadly things:
ticks, mosquitos, spiders, snakes.
At night the cicadas
are so loud they might
bust the window.
The frogs, they croak,
and I don't hear *ribbit.*
Instead, I hear,
Attack, attack, attack.

The Bodies That Fail Us

We decided that quarantine
would be fuckintine
except then I got a UTI

My political stance:
avoid antibiotics
at all costs

So I took cranberry, drank kefir,
it helped some,
the UTI would go away,

but it always came back.

Finally I called the doctor.
She was required to say
strange things
over the telephone. One was
that I could hang up anytime.

She called in two prescriptions.
Antibiotics, and the pills that make
your piss bright orange, extra strength.
I swallowed them. A little while later
I peed. So bright!
So bright. I felt powerful.

I have a highlighter
between my legs.

And One More For The Dog Parade

Yesterday I saw the most
majestic thing. I was standing
on my deck, listening to the scary
birds. I saw movement
in the trees, and then a tail.
It was four dogs,
identical in size,
but different breeds.
They were walking in a straight line
proud and slow,
navigating the curves
of the creek, all perfectly
equidistant from the other,
ears up.

They did not look at me but I still knew.
They were throwing me
a parade.

Who Is Responsible For My Emotional Problems?

hmmmm

not sure on that one

Marital Bed

He kept waking up in the night with my hands around his throat, strangling him. I was asleep while it happened, didn't remember it in the morning.

We went to the doctor. I changed into a paper gown while my husband sat anxiously on a chair. The doctor came in. His name was Dr. Specchio. He was wearing a white coat and glasses, and, on his forehead, an old fashioned head mirror. My husband told him what happened and the doctor murmured thoughtfully.

He listened to my breaths through a stethoscope. He looked in my ears, took my temperature. He left the room, came back.

"She has a demon," he said. His tone was so matter-of-fact that it felt scientific.

"Here is what you do," he said. "When she is menstruating, climb on her back while she is sleeping. Have intercourse with her from behind. Do not sleep in the same bed while she is not bleeding."

"How long should we do this?" I said.

"Indefinitely," he said.

"Indefinitely?" I said.

"Otherwise, she will continue to attack you and eventually she will succeed in killing you," he said to my husband.

I thought about the required sleeping arrangement. Maybe we could wedge a twin bed next to the wall.

"Can we sleep in the same room?" I asked.

The doctor shook his head. "I wouldn't," he said.

wading in a river in Nixa, MO. His death was "Undetermined" because De Leon also had a lethal level of oxycodone in his system, as well as nonlethal doses of alcohol and Vicodin.

1955, Billie's Cabaret, Baltimore. Frieda Hoxter, a German war bride, separated from her husband and began performing burlesque as "Princess Naja." She was bitten by one of two cobras she used in her performance, but continued dancing for eight more minutes. She was hospitalized at St. Joseph's Hospital, where she had been previously treated for snakebites, three times in three months. She died paralyzed in an iron lung.

Grant Thompson, 18, was found unresponsive in his car in a Lowe's parking lot in Austin, TX. A monocled cobra that he was known to own was missing. It was later found dead nearby, having been run over by a car. The death was ruled a suicide.

September 25, 1900: A newspaper article read: "Edward Comstock, manager of a snake show, was bitten by a rattlesnake at Chilll- cothe, O., last week and died, in terrible agony. His hand and arm swelled to an enormous size. Every known antidote was tried without avail. He had handled snakes for years."

North Dakota, 1913. Two Wilson children were bitten and died while their family was sleeping on the prairie.

Lightly Edited Selections From The "Fatal Snakebites In The United States" Wikipedia Page

George Yancy, 25, was bitten by a rattlesnake while pulling up his pants.

Brayden Bullard, of Bryceville, FL, was bitten by a rattlesnake while planting watermelons in his backyard. He was four years old.

Priscilla Meridith went to sit down in a friend's garden when she was bitten by a rattlesnake. She was not able to receive antivenom due to her allergies, which doctors said would have put her life at risk.

Joe Guidry, a fire marshal, went to help a neighbor who had spotted a rattlesnake while mowing his lawn. He shot at the snake; it went under a shed. Guidry was bitten when he reached for it.

Ernest Burch found a Timber rattlesnake in his garage in Armuchee, GA. Not wanting to kill it, he tried moving it out with a broom but lost his balance, fell on top of the snake, and was bitten on his left arm.

Alexandria Hall was bitten by a viper at her home and died two days later from a bleed in the brain.

Mark Randall Wolford, a pastor, was bitten on the thigh while handling a timber rattlesnake as part of a religious service in McDowell County, WV. Wolford's father, Mack, died in 1983 under similar circumstances.

John Wayne "Punkin" Brown, a pastor, had reportedly survived 22 snake bites. On October 3, 1998, he was bitten by a rattlesnake during a religious service. Punkin's wife, Melinda, had been killed by a snake in similar circumstances three years earlier. They left five children orphaned.

Gilbert De Leon, 37, was bitten by a cottonmouth on each leg while

Ode IX: Bloodline

For Iris McClanahan

But my favorite writer is a twelve-year-
Old girl whose hair is always a giant
Mess and I try to brush out the tangles
And you yell at me. I try very hard
Not to hurt you. Your big eyes and your hard
Forehead, long legs make it impossible
To share a bed with you. I wait til you
Fall asleep and then I sneak out. You are
Always saying that you are a girly
Girl. We might have different definitions
But that is not how I see you and I
Tell you this, which makes you angry, but all
I mean is you are not precious, you are
A gold streak crash on the world a lightning
Bolt, formidable. You once called me your
Rival. Now, we are mirrors, and I want your
Version of the world to be real, your big
Dreams, your small ones, all the children that live
In your head and their names, careful birth dates.
At the same age we both loved the same book,
The one for little girls that is about
Illness, Hitler and fear. I think about
The space you take in my life, the space I
Take in yours and it is impossible
To not believe in God, the angels lined
Us up to find each other, it can't be
Dumb luck. And now our stories are so twined
Together. My trail, faint splotches, but yours
In bold. Please pick up and cradle my bones.

Ode VIII: McDonald's Is Impossible

For Chelsea Martin

We talked in the mall. I thought you hated
Me. We talked in the bookstore and I thought
You hated me. You didn't hate me. You
Just aren't good at modulating your voice.
Well, neither am I. Two monotone lumps.

I miss you living in the cold state that
Made your nose bleed. Now you live somewhere else,
Too far away, both of us far flung in
These stupid places, regional airports,
So expensive to fly on a plane! In
This economy! My husband has a

Story about you wandering around
San Francisco and how you kept asking
Him, a drunk, if you had a stye in your
Eye. That tour is the first time I met you,
After watching you on the internet,
I copied your videos. You are the
Originator of all that was cool
Then, all that is cool now, saying you would
Rather fuck William H. Macy. And yes,
You're right, about everything, yes, Scott's clothes,
Dirty, chicken wings. Little bitch. I love

It when you smile, and I love how soft
And sweet you are, thoughtful, and how you hide
That, or at least hid, past tense, I don't know,
Maybe you're different now. Now that you have
The baby, the boy who needs you. Life,
It changes things.

Ode VII: Glitter Fist

For Amanda McNeil

I want to put you in a silent film
White skin, rosebud mouth, pre-Raphaelite hair
Watch your big round eyes playact fright at a
Train, wrists bound to the tracks and you writhing.

You live in my mind before the pretty
River that runs with chemicals and drugs.
Somebody famous on it but I can't
Remember who. I want to say Mark Twain
But that's wrong. You told a story about
Fisting to the cute Christian grandparents,
A parable, except they weren't that kind
Of Christian. They liked hearing about lubed
Fists shoved inside butts. And the sadness in

Your eyes is melted warm like chocolate smudge,
You make fun, you know that all jokes stem from
A well of tragedy, and you've got a
Whole bucket. You love your ugly dog and
I love the things you make with your hands, how
They all sparkle and I picture you with
A smear of glitter across your pink mouth

Not let things go if you love them, wrap them
In a napkin, stick them in your purse, tucked
In bed, loved like kittens, blessing their hearts,
You Baptist. You baptizer.

Ode VI: Leo Queen

For Ashleigh Bryant Phillips

You are a Leo, born in the tail end
Of summer, hair a gold spun cloud around
Your head. Jewel eyes shine regal above
The peaks of your cheeks. You wear

The red dress, velvet pours to the floor, pinched
In a heart above your breast. You tell us
About the cousin from whom you got it
And each turn becomes more fantastical—
Her lovers, her wedding in Europe, the
Way you convinced everybody to let
You go, have your dreams fulfilled. And that is
You. You bend the world in your will, tie the
Ribbons into stories, twist a spatter
Of dots, spin it into lore, a detail

Noticer. Another evening, hotel
Room, your eyes, flashing and aglow, find the
Funny things of existence, unafraid
To attack it with talons. And one thing
I love is your love of small things. You point
Out scents and textures, excited at the
Existence of a menu, a new thing
To order, a list to check off. And I

Wish I could see you walking the roads of
Woodlawn. In my mind they are dusty, looped
In kudzu, paint peeled and shabby, the way
They are in the town where I live. I want
To see that town the way you see it, shaped
In your hand, features plucked through until the
Blurred outlines suck in the light and glow
Morbidly with color. The way you will

It's funny but when I think of you
I don't see those orb eyes, the scars, the lips.
I think of your smile, which is a little
Goofy, and the softness of it, it makes
me just
ache

Ode V: Flowers And Faygo

For Elle Nash

The first time I meet you, at that woman's
House, the one we've all written off since, you're
Ethereal, electric crackle, wrapped
Up in the flimsy gauze of this earth. And

The thing you want to hide is the thing I
Find most beautiful, scars on your thighs, scars
On your cheeks, white streaks to prove you are
Alive, human, here, in spite of it all.

When I am near you, it feels like you could
Shatter with a slight bit of pressure kicked
In the wrong place, and it makes me want to
Envelop you, this animal princess.

Which is all completely ridiculous
Because you are not fragile, because you
Are fearless, a banshee, with your dagger,
Your blood, your black clothes and your Faygo.

The way you say you are going to do
Big scary things and then you just do them.
You just move, to the mountains, across the
Ocean, have a baby, stick needles in

Strange arms, stab your face, quit your job. You
Make it look easy, just do it, just like
That. And you aren't afraid of the mud of
The mind, roll around in it, spin it like
Sheen into beauty. The animals and
The pixels and your own polished gloss, lips
Puffed into rosebud, hair always changing.

Too swept by joy to notice. I ask You
What a dream means and You tell me only
I can give it meaning. You go dark and
Live, guilty, in a blue space on my phone.

Ode IV: The Book Of Megan

For Megan Boyle

Impossible to speak of you without
Superlatives. Most kind most open most
Accepting. The softness of You and the
Ease of Your affection, the way strangers
Always tell You their stories. You are not
Meant for constraint. Your form fills the thousand
Page bible You wrote, the Book of Megan.

The nights on Skype, late for me, later for
You, fallow days of that bible, no sleep,
You, trapped in a tiny box on my desk,
Long hair falls, a thick curtain for small birds
To take roost in, you, who always smells good,
Verdant, blooms tilt in your mouth, your corners,
Adorned in pretty things, rocks, old photos,
Your mastery of light and color. But
Your purse—complete and utter disaster.

And it's always been easy to talk to
You about pain. And also, we're in love
With absurdity—O life! What if we
Could only could never. Remember when
You gave me Covid, sharing pastries and
Fruit, at the old hotel named for a dead
Socialite? Maybe You didn't get me
Sick. But I want it to be You. You, who
Made me hack disease on the Mennonites.

And remember on Your wedding? How it
Rained? And You didn't care about Your hair?
How the woman from the gallery kept
Reminding You to hold the umbrella
But You wouldn't? You let the rain fall wet,

Ode III: Crazy Eyes

For Daisuke Shen

We met over Zoom, the height of the pandemic,
And you said something about being manic.
Internally, I rolled my eyes, here we go again,
Another "bipolar" person, another "manic episode,"
The terminal uniqueness of the perpetually online.
But then I watched your eyes. In them, I saw the
Divine presence of God. I recognized the
Tilting dark disc. You were really crazy.
The real deal. We became friends.

And we spoke about those "Crazy eyes,"
The pupils, they dilate, attract strange
Creatures in the street. It is easy to eat a pill
And it is easy to smile but there is nothing
One can do to hide the eyes.

In person, I meet you in the crowded bar,
And you flit over to me. Your body is still
But there is a tremble in your quick,
Like a plant, something living
And fertile yet fragile. You hand

Me a present, a cloth, not a scarf, and I
Take it home, take it in the woods,
I pick flowers, wrap them in it. I put them
In a vase and some of the flowers wilt easy
But the ironweed stays strong,
Streaks of purple for weeks.

Ode II: Manson Girl

For Mesha Maren

I want to see the child, the closeted queer,
Raised among cows, well water and mud,
Her mind wild with poems and the moon.

You rarely talk about yourself, secret
Life, what you were doing in Mexico,
How well you speak Spanish, why you

Became a stripper or why you stopped. But
I do love the story of your mother,
Cutting off her finger the blood spilled,

With no chance for ambulance. Your birth, made
Possible by Squeaky Fromme, her escape art,
The prison camp, hair flaming red like yours.

Thoughts skid across eyelids. I see you
At the top of the mountain, Muddy Creek,
Long grass, the rich wet of the air, your promised land.

Eastern Greenbrier, yet you could be at home
In a Western. I see your braid, back in sheepskin, sharp
Knife, hands pounding bread and, if needed, a wolf.

One time I asked you how to win prizes
You said it was easy. Pretend they are
Men. Pretend they are men who want to give
Dollar bills. And I envied your
Complexity, your adeptness at nuance.

Ode I: Lamb's Ear

For Nicolette Polek

For you, the world is not a dead dullard.
Each day a practice for the sacred act
Of noticing, each small thing holding the
Volume for wonder. In the forest you
Touch the mushrooms and your head is filled with
Angels, when so much else has killed, vacant.

Two sides to you, one with the grace tawdry
Americans lack, the first time we met
On the train, thin fingers grasping the pole,
Constrained at your center, sharp cheeks, pink mouth.
Oftentimes, to hear you, one must lean in.
Your voice, timid animal, requiring

Faith earned and a stillness. The other side,
The child waits in the hall, library,
Piano lessons, obscure games, nerdy,
Two parents on a lone planet with bugs.
Each half bursts the whole to make you. After
The wedding, you stop on the walk at the

Lamb's ear, growing between the roses, with
Beads of rain like jewels caught along the down.
We touch them and they leak on our fingers.

INTERLUDE

couldn't be bothered to eat and nothing seemed to matter but I did my homework anyway.

Then it got to be summer. I've always been sensitive to seasons, to the turns of the moon. I stopped needing to sleep again. I drove from college back to home after finals. It was so sunny. It was so warm. I was listening to T. Rex in the car, and the music sounded so good.

Things went bad after that. I got real skinny, I couldn't stop talking, and my heart was always pounding, pounding, pounding, ticking off time like a clock. The look in my eyes became glinty and sharp.

I drank a lot, to bring myself down. I'd drive my car real fast, especially at dawn. You can't get a DUI when you're driving drunk in the day. The signs on the freeway fly by when you're driving like that. The lines in the road look like snakes, and it becomes so easy to imagine yourself crashing right into a cement wall – bam – and then blood.

X

This was right before I got clean, but I didn't know that yet. I was drinking too much again, every night, every day. Everything blended together. The pills, too, they coated things like my life was behind greasy glass. The ones I took, they were things people don't talk about abusing too much: Methadone, Restoril. You can snort the Restoril but you have to swallow the Methadone. It's a big pill, sometimes gets caught in your throat.

I'd get drunk at the bar with my friends and then I'd drive myself home. That was when I took the pills. I lay around, slumped against the wall, flat on the ground, flat on my back. Everything turns liquid when you get that high. Sometimes, for a moment, I could feel my heart stop.

alien problem was real bad here, what with all the military bases. That's why the helicopters flew over so often at night. They were telling the aliens: Look at my big ass jet plane. I'll fucking shoot you.

I learned all about the aliens at the library. I learned about the crop circles too. Aliens liked pyramids, apparently. I liked pyramids, so I carved one into my thigh. People are so fucking stupid. They say cutting is for attention, it stems from pain, it points to a hatred of self. But sometimes you just want to make something on yourself that will never go away, something you shaped, something that will be there forever: a sign for someone else to find.

VIII

I couldn't stop doing coke all the time. I hated it, but I just couldn't stop. My nose would bleed, but still I did it while driving, putting it up my nose in one of those plastic bullet things. I did it off the toilet tank at work. I did it at home, with my boyfriend, with my friend, with our friends, alone. Off CDs and the coffee table, off notebooks and my desk and the bathroom counter and of course I once snorted it off my boyfriend's hard dick. Every night, the dark would creep into day and the birds would start chirping and the planes would start flying overhead again – we lived right under the path of the airport – and my head would ache, my whole face hurt. In bed, my boyfriend would try and lean his body into mine but I couldn't let him. I couldn't let anyone touch me. I just wanted to be left alone to hurt. One morning he asked me why I wouldn't let him hold me, over and over, until I got up and punched the window. It cut through my skin, on the wrist. Looked like a bad suicide attempt, like I tried to go across the street instead of down.

IX

I stopped taking medication my junior year of college. Decided that "bipolar" was something "made up" to explain away the anger and drugs. At first it was okay, I was just depressed. I'd sleep all day and he stapled it up. There were twelve of them, twelve staples. When I got back to school, the kids said it looked like Frankenstein.

VI

I got out of the school and started dating this guy. It happened because we were both on acid and he had vines growing out of his head and looked like Mowgli. I licked him on the nose and the next thing I knew we were fucking in his backyard.

It was a bad relationship. There was no other way to look at it. We fought right from the start. We kept on breaking up and getting back together. We kept on getting too fucked up, and he kept on breaking my things. He kicked my car door in. He stomped on my purse and broke my pager and make-up. One time I yelled at him and he grabbed my arm and threw me against the wall. In the morning, there were four fingerprint bruises on the white part of my arm, lined up in a row like stones.

It took two years for us to break up for good. What did it was him chasing me around the house with a kitchen knife, saying he was going to slit my throat. I'm pretty sure he was just being dramatic, but it was hard to tell. I called the cops. He left while I was on the phone. I didn't see him after that.

VII

I couldn't sleep again. In the mornings, out of boredom, I went to the library.

I would only look at books about aliens and crop circles. I wasn't too sure about aliens before, but recently I'd risen into a new clarity. The

During the day I got mad and yelled a lot. I broke things. Dishes. The faucet. I threw a glass of milk at a counselor's head once, but I missed.

We were supposed to go snowboarding. I was excited. I was thinking about snorting the Adderall in the bathroom and how fun it would be to fly down the hill. But then the headmaster said she had to talk to me. She told me I couldn't go snowboarding. I got mad.

I went into my bedroom and slammed the door. There was a razor hidden in my sock drawer. I wasn't supposed to have regular razors, I was supposed to use electric only because I was a "cutter," but other girls had them so I'd stolen some. I ripped the head off, put it in my mouth, and bit down until the blades separated from the plastic. Sometimes this cut my mouth up but usually it didn't. The blades were good this way: thin, sharp, and flexible. But you had to be careful, to not cut too deep, and I wasn't careful this time. My hands were shaking. I hadn't slept in so long.

I cut open my arm, dragging the razor, and then made two more cuts, quick ones. The first was the deepest. It was getting all bloody now. I picked up a sock, to wipe it off, but it just made more of a mess. I took the bloody sock and tried to make a tourniquet, but my arm kept right on with the bleeding. It was doing the pulsing thing, where the blood escapes from your body at the same rate as the beat of your heart. It was getting everywhere now. I didn't know what to do about it.

I went back into the living room and the headmaster was there with the other kids and Janice the counselor and they were all like, Oh my god. Janice took me to the clinic. It was twenty miles out, and I just bled and bled the whole way in the van, soaking through two hand towels. The doctor stuck a needle in my arm and numbed it real good and then

embarrassed and afraid so I said nothing and walked out.

IV

I got diagnosed right after that. They gave me a lot of pills: one red, one yellow, three whites. Five pills every morning. Five pills is a lot to swallow.

A few weeks later, and I was walking home. I took a shortcut through a field, and the sky was a strange color, not blue but also not grey – kind of yellow. There were crows flying around, making their squawk noises and flapping. The world was about to dissolve, they told me this, and it was my fault. I believed them.

I went home and took the pill bottles and emptied them on top of my math book. I poured a big glass of gin. It looked like water. I swallowed a handful of pills with a big gulp of gin, and did it again and again until there was nothing left. PJ Harvey was playing. I woke up in the hospital three days later. A machine had done the breathing for me and now I couldn't talk.

V

I had a boyfriend at the school for kids with problems. He gave me his Adderall because he didn't like it. I liked the Adderall. I liked to crush it up and snort it.

Instead of sleeping at night I read books from the office about mental illness and the medications they give the mentally ill. I learned they didn't know much of anything; everything they did to us was all trial and error, mostly error. I didn't sleep and didn't sleep and instead I read and read.

instead I smoked weed in the canyon or went to the house of the boyfriend that lived down the block.

One day we were sitting in the garage, bored. The other boyfriend was there too. There was beer. We drank it. It was warm. There was a Guns N' Roses poster on the wall, and Axl looked sexy in it.

"We should have a threesome," one of the boyfriends said.

"Yeah," said the other.

"Okay," I said.

They looked surprised. I felt surprised myself, but I also felt like I couldn't take back what I said.

I watched them as they took off their pants and rolled on condoms. The skin underneath was so white. They came over to me, and one of them kissed me while the other took off my jeans. One of them put his dick in me. The other one put his dick in my mouth. It didn't feel good and it didn't feel bad. I looked up at Axl. I looked up at them. We were action figures, or Barbies, and someone was playing with us just to see what we could do. I laughed, with the dick still in my mouth. The boyfriends laughed too. It was like we were sharing a joke but I guess in some ways it wasn't funny at all.

III

I was sixteen and in biology class. The teacher was talking about Punnett squares. There were pink and white and red flowers on the overhead, each of them with four petals. I looked away from the projector and there was this big skull floating out of the wall, surrounded by smaller ones. I knew they weren't real but they scared me anyway, because they were there and because they were shadowy and dark. I got up and went to the door. The teacher asked where I was going. I felt

Trouble and Troubledness

I

My dad gave me a pocketknife for my eleventh birthday. It had my name on the side and came with tweezers that looked like barbeque tongs for dolls.

One day my mom yelled at me for something that made no sense and so I ran outside. The thing swirled up, the empty black thing, growing from the pit of my stomach, tendrils reaching into my arms. My vision went hot and I wanted to jump into the ocean and swim out far until I couldn't come back.

I flicked the blade out. I wanted to make a heart in my calf. My skin got whiter as I cut, and then the whiteness filled in with blood. I carved each line three times, just to make sure it went deep enough. The blackness shrank.

I wiped the blood away with the meaty part of my palm. I licked my hand clean. It tasted like copper and dirt. My leg hurt, but I felt tough on the inside, like I could hide the thing inside me. My jeans stuck to the blood but later it scabbed over, and when the scab fell off there was a perfect and even heart-shaped scar.

II

When I was fifteen, I had two best friends. They had boyfriends who were also best friends. I had no boyfriend. My friends were sometimes mean to me.

The best friends went away for Christmas. The boyfriends and I stayed in town. I spent the evenings sitting around listening to The Doors. During the day I told my mom I was going to the beach, but much more solid. It felt good to conjure; it felt good to finally, for once, have some power. I said her name again, and then her fine blond hair blew upwards in the wind. "Why won't you leave us alone?" Her form was fading and it was starting to rain.

It was just me and her grave then. There was dirt on the stone marker, and I scuffed it away with my foot. I still couldn't figure out why she fucking cared.

I woke up right after, and Caleb was curling his sleep-hot body into mine. The light from the dawn made our room streaked with shadows and the darkness licked us, lying together in our bed. He looked so peaceful when he was sleeping, so small, that I thought maybe I could break him apart.

My knuckles were bleeding. "It fell off the wall. Cut myself when I went to pick it up."

He acted polite and pretended I wasn't lying.

We went to sleep, together but alone, that night. We did no eye gazing at all. Just stared at the backs of our own eyelids, an act that doesn't take and gives nothing to no one.

***

Charlotte came to me in a dream, again. She'd been doing that for a while, but usually I just ignored her. Tonight, she was all white gown and washed-out skin. Like she was dead. We were in Queens and there was a spit of whiskey on her grave. The liquor hung heavy in the air.

"What do you want?" I said, not accusatory, just wondering.

Charlotte gripped me by the shoulders and her touch was cold and then she brought her face to mine. "What are you so afraid of?" she asked me.

I was quiet because I knew she really was asking for an answer, and I had to think. *Everything*, I wanted to say, *it's everything in this world that scares me,* but I knew how dumb that sounded.

Except she was a ghost, so I only needed to say the words in my head. Charlotte laughed, all metallic and light. "That's funny," she said. "He's afraid of everything too." She smiled at me. I'd never seen a smile so warm, especially coming off a dead girl.

"Charlotte," I said, and by saying her name, her form became that

But if that isn't love, well then I don't know what is. I couldn't bring myself to tell him the truth, that all that darting around had nothing to do with wildness. It was as simple as knowing he'd break *me*. I hadn't the magic to do that kind of thing to him.

The next day, after he'd left for work, I looked in the mirror just to check. There was no wildness. There was no power. There was only greyness, my heart stifled, my expression rolling out flat.

The girl on the train, the one that looked like Charlotte, was humming a little tune. I wondered if it was what Caleb sang to her, and if they'd sung it together. It was a nice tune. I might like to hum it myself but I'm tone deaf.

Charlotte's nail polish matched her lipstick, and her purse matched her shoes. My nail polish was chipped, and my shoes had busted soles and matched nothing. I wondered what would happen if I told her to shut up.

She got off at the next stop: Wall Street. Charlotte was probably a banker – would explain the fancy shoes – not some perpetually broke English teacher like me.

***

I was so mad that night when Caleb got home, but he just smiled and stared and pretended nothing was wrong. We drank wine and I drank too much. At one point, I really did feel wild eyed. I went into the bathroom while he was turning the record to take a look at myself, so empty and wanting, and then I punched the mirror.

Caleb came running. "What happened?" he said.

to like the way I sang. I spat whiskey on her grave and then I sat against the tree and cried."

"You never sing me songs," I said.
"You never asked me to."
And that was that. And then we had dinner.

***

The next day on the subway, I was going to work and someone sat beside me, someone that looked like her. Charlotte. Same long limbs and same fine hair, same slight smile and same blue eyes, just like I'd seen in the pictures. She sat there next to me, the vibrancy around her humming and doing tricks. This was a nice girl, all clear skin and clean clothes. This was a woman who was nothing like me. She looked whole and she looked happy, and here I was, late for work and neither.

Sometimes I felt I wasn't enough for Caleb, but then I'd remember when we met he'd stare at me for hours, looking in my eyes like he was taking something from me. Sometimes I'd stir in my sleep, even now, and he'd be sitting there and just watching. "You look so peaceful when you're sleeping," he said the first time I caught him.

"And awake?"

"When you're awake," he said, "your eyes are wild." He took my hand, the way he does when he has to tell me some truth. "They dart about and don't ever stop on something for too long, like you're afraid that by looking at things you could break them apart. You could break me apart." He kissed me on the cheek, all tender like he does, and the whole thing was so sweet I wanted to puke.

Here is a Ghost Story

My boyfriend's fiancée is dead. Charlotte is her name. She's been dead long before I met Caleb, but still she comes around.

Yesterday was All Soul's Day, so he went out to the graveyard in Queens to pay his respect. It was cold, one of those days with the sky so grey it looks like it's been baked in lint. The kind that confines you, makes it hard to breathe. The trees hang crooked and thin this time of year.

I wasn't invited, so I lay out on the couch while he was gone, listening to sad songs and smoking cigarettes. Seemed a good time to honor my losses, too.

When Caleb came back, the room was dark and the needle was skating the edge of the record. "That wears it down," he scolded me, as he'd done so many times before.

"Sorry," I told him, but I wasn't. I liked the sound of a spinning record. Reminds you things still go around – endless circles, endless chain – even when you think they aren't meant to.

He sat down on the coffee table in front of me. I hadn't yet bothered to get up. He still hadn't taken off his gloves, and there was mud on his boots.

"So," he said, but really what he meant was *What the fuck are you doing?* because I was just sitting there, alone in the dark.

"So," I said, ignoring what he didn't say. "How was it?"

He looked up real quick and then went somewhere far away in his head. When he came back, he said, "I sang songs to her, cus she used

"Let's go," I said, and grabbed his hand. "Grunion run."

We ran to the shore, our fingers interlaced, and my heart leapt because I felt like one half of a normal couple. I watched him carefully as the fish fucked slippery between our toes. The cuffs of my jeans grew heavy and wet, and the good man laughed and laughed. I relaxed. He was safe. I couldn't get to him. There was hope for us yet.

I plunged my hand into the darkness and extracted a fish. It flopped around in my palm, telling my fortune like a red piece of Chinese plastic film. If the fish turns over, it means your heart is fickle. Stay on one side, I told the fish, stay true. I stared at it in the moonlight, its flat-looking moon eyes, its leg-looking little fins. I closed my hand around it again, felt the solidness of this fish, felt myself grow lost in the blackness of its gaze. Then its eyes and mine became one. The fish stilled in my hand.

The ground grew unsteady. I didn't know where it was safe to plant my feet. I felt the world under the sand opening from below, vast and ugly and so incomprehensibly dark.

When I looked up again, there was a flash of brightness on the horizon. I saw the good man's shoulders above the water, outlined by the light. Then I only saw his head, and then he was gone.

it's called. Living light. Fireflies and jellyfish do it too, but this is better, this is the sea itself, it is more powerful. But sometimes it glows too strong and the surfers can't help but follow it under. Sometimes they dive down and sometimes they die."

I wanted to stop speaking now, but I had already gone too far. The words tumbled out of my mouth in ribbons, bitter and curling. I watched his eyes glaze over as I spoke. I watched his pupils turn into flat disks, dull and dry as paper.

I was quiet. I was worried. His breathing was heavy and deep. I hadn't wanted to do this, to say those things, but, like always, it just sort of happened. Time passed, and I let it. Slowly, the good man's breaths returned to normal.

"Where did you hear this?" he asked me, finally.

His pupils looked alright again. I inhaled sharp, a sigh of relief.

"My mother," I said to him. "She's a Marine Biologist," I lied.

"She compared the water to blood?" he said. "She told you surfers die looking for light?"

"Blood's what it looks like," I said, and took a sip of wine, "and it's true." I closed my eyes, but the moon still glowed through the backs of my eyelids, seared in like a stamp.

He kissed me, and I kissed back. I slid off my jeans. Like with most good men, the act was unremarkable. I was pleased, though, because that meant I hadn't gotten into him. Perhaps he was stronger than I thought. Perhaps his goodness was rooted more firmly than the blackness in my words.

It was fully dark now, and the light glistened pale on the flat waves. I could see the fish had come in by the way the light darted off of the water.

Grunion Run

We decided to watch the fish fuck on the beach. It was my first date with this good man, and the moon was waning gibbous. I should have read the signs, yet still I was hopeful. Before I met up with him, I coached myself: This is a good man, so I will be good; no trouble, no trickery, no vexes.

We met at the beach at sunset. He brought a blanket, a chocolate bar, and a bottle of wine. We sat in the sand and began to drink. The sun sank down and the air grew cold and he held my hand. He told me about his day, he told me sweet things, and quickly I grew bored and restless. So I started telling him things my mother taught me while I was growing up.

"The sand will be alive soon, and slippery," I started, because that's what my mother told me to say. "It will crawl, and you won't know where to stand, where it will be safe to plant your feet. The ground will move under you, you will no longer mistake it for a solid object. The air will stink strongly of fish."

He smiled politely, pretended as though I wasn't speaking in incantations. He was new to California, moved here three months ago from the Midwest, so it was alright for me to talk in this way. California is the last place on the map, land of golden dreams, and I wanted to be a dreamer. He may have been a good man, but I knew he still wanted a little magic.

"This isn't the only strange thing the ocean does," I continued. "On the right nights, the sun falls into the horizon like Achilles and flashes green. Sometimes the waves turn thick and brown with algae, it looks like rusted blood, and the city quarantines off the beach from hopeful swimmers. But once it is dark, the surfers sneak out anyway and the crests of the waves glint blue beneath their boards. Bioluminescence,

"Here," he says.

He turns around on his stool, so we are no longer facing the door and the bar. Now no one can look at our faces. We close our eyes, and we breathe deep.

At first it is nothing, and then it is something and then it feels like I'm floating. It feels so good that I do not question if these feelings are real and valid, or if there is simply too much dopamine sizzling around in my brain. I feel like the burden of being troubled, of being human, has been lifted, and I let it lift. I let myself sit there with my eyes closed, just breathing. I let myself feel like a cobalt blue ball.

harder than it sounds but it's easier than you might think.

He let me live with him for three months once, back when I got fired and had no money saved, at a time when I had nowhere to go. On one of those nights, I came home with a busted lip and no bag of coke. Zachary went out and found my coke dealer, took a bat and beat him up.

The kava works and I love it – I love that it calms me – and I love that it comes with a chaser. I love the kava bar, too, despite and maybe because the inside of it is made to look like a tree. When I go to the bathroom, I see a cobalt blue ball hovering in the air, and it glows with something that might be love. I tell myself it is not the mania, it is not the kava, it is the truth and it is real.

There is a yoga class going on in the back of the room; the class is breathing deeply and there are weird chants going on. I tell Zachary that this is all too spiritual for me. He looks at me in a way that tells me he used to think that too. Zachary has been busy changing, it seems. Old Zachary would never hang out in a kava bar. But the old me wouldn't, either.

A few minutes later, and the chants go away. A new track begins on the stereo system.

"This is my jam," Zachary says to me.

"Seriously?" I say.

"Seriously," he says. "If you close your eyes, you feel like you're floating."

I close my eyes, for a second, but there's people in the room and daylight through the door and so they flicker back open. "I want to close my eyes," I tell him. "But I feel too self-conscious."

This process repeated itself, until one day it stopped. This was all a long time ago. This was back when we were different people.

I once asked Zachary if the fiancée knew that we used to sleep together. He says he thinks she knows but doesn't want to know. Personally, my favorite method for treating our history is to pretend it doesn't exist. Usually it feels like it doesn't.

The kava bartender, who has tinged blue hair and the eyes to match, tells me her spiel about the kava. It tastes like dirt water, is made from the root, and grows in places like Fiji. It does good things: relaxes muscles, calms you down and makes you feel happy. These cups are made from coconut shells. We should cheers them together and we should say "Bula." The slices of orange are the chaser.

Zachary says "Bula," but that seems like bullshit so I say nothing, and we clink the coconut shells together. We drink the kava. We suck on the oranges. We wait.

I was scared to drink the kava because I had never done it before and because I knew I would like it because it will change how I feel. But Zachary peer pressured me into coming here. Which is funny, considering when I had one year sober, he called me and told me he would send me heroin in the mail because he knew it would turn me into a junkie, like him. I hung up on him and started to cry. This was the last time we talked until he got clean again.

It is not fair, to Zachary, to tell you that story, without telling you that he was instrumental in getting me clean and helping me stay that way – despite and maybe because of the phone call about heroin. When I got sober, my thoughts would get to churning and until nothing made sense anymore. "Stop thinking," he would tell me, so I stopped. It worked. It's

I Do Not Question It

I am sitting in the kava bar with Zachary. We have not seen each other in six months, even though he is one of my best friends, even though we once again live in the same city. I tell myself this is because he just broke up with his fiancée and we are only there for each other when we need it, but this isn't entirely true. It is also because he hates making plans and I operate only on a schedule. But my schedule has been torn down because right now, I can only take each day as it comes.

One month ago, I had my first appointment with a shit psychiatrist, but I didn't know he was shit yet. Nineteen days ago, I started losing my mind even worse. Two weeks ago, I was in the emergency room, getting sedated because I thought I could see god and I was swearing at her, calling her a dumb bitch and worse things. Three days ago, Zachary got dumped by his girlfriend. Two days ago, and Zachary moved in with me. Four years ago, I got sober. One year after that, Zachary relapsed on heroin, a slide that began with a doctor stupid enough to feed him Xanax. It took two more years for him to get clean.

We've switched places with who's crazier so many times, first me and them him and then me, but right now it's hard to see the difference. We're both sedated – Zachary on Thorazine, temporarily, for the break up; me on Seroquel, long term, for being insane – but the drugs only blot away so much of the glow.

Our friendship is strange and it deserves a story of its own. How we met deserves a story of its own, too, but I will sketch it here briefly because it will help you understand. We met when we were both very fucked up, in many different ways. Think of all the ways a person can be fucked up, and there – you pretty much have it. We had the kind of sex that is both very intimate and very cold, the kind that leaves marks, and then we stopped talking. Later, like weeks later, and we began to text each other mean and hateful things. The hateful texts led to more sex.

The train comes but it has the wrong number on the front and I move myself to the middle of the platform, because suddenly I realize how beautiful it would be to jump. If there were swords in stones with the pricks facing outwards, I would surely hurl my heart at one, just to try it, just to say that I did. To see what it feels like to have something slice me open.

The feeling I have, the flutter in my chest – this has nothing to do with being suicidal. I don't want to die. I don't even want to close my eyes. It's more like this world is not enough for me. I have too much in my heart to be in it.

I don't know what I should do with this, with the boiling going on inside my head. I tell myself it's not real, these are just thoughts, but I fear I might do something stupid. As explosive as I feel, it is nice, too, because I feel like I'm holding onto a secret. I will sit here and brace myself, my knuckles white as my insides burn, and no one will know this fire.

The train comes, and I get on, and the people inside are all quiet. I want to scream at them, to let them know, to show them just what I've found:

That you should cut these strings.
You should cut me open.
You should hunt and slay
my pink thudding heart.

Your eyes may not show it,
they might not burn with my fever
but your chest holds one, too.

LET IT OUT.

Mental Illness on a Weekday

These days, and I do what I should. I eat breakfast, I get enough sleep, I wash my hair. When I'm troubled I tell someone who has felt like me. When I'm agitated I close my eyes, take deep breaths, and treat my thoughts like clouds. I don't do drugs anymore, even though sometimes I'd like to. I have a man who loves me, and I've never thrown anything at this one, besides a bucket or two of sharp words.

Sometimes, still though, things line up in an odd way; maybe it's the shifting of the planets or moon. The chemicals become unbalanced, and like a scale, I can feel it. The weight shifts around on the platform and I become unglued.

In the mirror, my pupils are wet and black like a lake. My thoughts come quick and brilliant, too painful to take in at once. I want to argue about unarguable things, like the Nature of Society and God. No one will win. I can't sleep without the pills.

In the morning, the brilliance is gone and all that remains is the hard, fragile edges. My insides feel smoky. I break the lamp, but that was an accident.

I enter the subway. I'd like to let myself boil over, rip open my chest, but people expect so much of me and there's no room in this world to let it go. I am afraid, because I want to do something questionable. I want to steal from you, to break you, I want to kiss you on the cheek and punch your quiet mouth. I want to fuck that man at my work, the mean one with the bad hair, who tempts me because I know he is bad, just so I could ruin the heart of the man who gives himself to me. I tell myself it is because my boyfriend doesn't understand what I go through, not really, but this is a lie; the bad man understands me much less.

paned, but it still felt bone-cold. You struck a match, held it up to crumpled newspaper.

"So what do I do?" I said. My time clean was short enough that life fucked up still felt very close. I remembered it clearly, a lot more clearly than I had when I was drinking, and I was willing to do anything to keep it at bay.

You smiled. "Go where it's warm," you said, rubbing your hands in front of your new fire. "Meetings. Safe spots. Places with me."

The city was gray beneath me: the sky, the buildings, the streets, the water. I could almost see the death on each whitecap in the choppy tips of the river, the way the city and the winter called to those who might want to die. Each building held a secret, a bar, a drug, an addict. A potential death that wanted to happen. But the cold inside me—I could feel it beginning to melt. It hurt, the way my hands hurt when I've been out in the snow with no gloves and I come inside and it feels like they're on fire.

"Come sit by me," you said. "Come sit by the fire."

Your eyes glowed with fever; your hands open and out, wanting me. Fifteen years sober and yet you were still sick and desperate. It was all the same, but now your drug had a pulse.

So I took your hand and I held it for a moment, but then I let it go.

Hurricane Season

Itchy in November, right before Thanksgiving. It was my first winter sober, when you were living on the top floor of that six-story apartment building overlooking the river, back before the neighborhood was converted into condos.

"Hurricane season," you said when you saw me looking out your window in that blank way. "When the temperatures drop, us drunks get restless."

Your hands got busy stacking up wood in the fireplace. I'd seen people who had come into the same meetings every week suddenly stop showing up, seen the way that the ones who did come back would raise their hands, announcing their day counts, differently this time. "I've got five days." "Nineteen days." "I've got forty-one days back," they'd say, the "back" added to show that this wasn't their first time at the rodeo. It didn't look like it was any easier, though: their hands shook like any newcomer's, their eyes wandered the rooms the same way, rabid.

I still didn't know anyone in those days, so I couldn't ask them why they left, or how it felt to come back. I wouldn't have known about what was going on at all if you hadn't explained it to me. You said that no one talked to me because they were jealous that I was pretty, but that didn't make sense to me, not even then. There were other pretty girls in the program, and they had friends. I thought the difference between me and them must have been you. Well, at least, that you didn't help. But it must have looked worse from your corner: you were twice my age, with fifteen years of sobriety, yet you were there dating me, the fragile newcomer. You always swore up and down that this was the first time you'd done such a thing, but I doubted you. Doubted that this was your first time with the so-called thirteenth step—the one where you initiate a newcomer by fucking them.

I pressed my fingers against the glass. Your window was double-high making words proves more of an effort than it's worth.

One day we decided to do an experiment. I was at school, and, like usual, Adam went to Mike's after he got off work. I was tired when I got home but felt better when I saw the little baggies sitting there on our coffee table, the tiny crystals just gleaming and waiting. Except there was another bag too, this one pinkie mice, their flesh wrinkled and naked, tiny eyes still shut into slits. Adam said he wanted to try feeding them to the fish. Said he'd read on the internet that sometimes puffers were into that kind of thing, that this type of fish had teeth.

We smoked the stuff, and I settled back into my bones again. Adam let me dangle the first mouse above the water. He sat next to me, his knee pressing into my thigh.

The fish swam up. The cichlids were first, and they sniffed but then quickly darted away, bored. The puffers, though – they knew what was going on. One nibbled delicately, first at the tail and then at the arm. The mouse hung there, suspended in my fingers, pale trails of blood trickling into the water from where the limbs used to be. The baldness, the incompleteness, reminded me of Mike. Suddenly I almost wished he was here, telling us sad stories and cupping his incomplete wrist.

Soon the other fish smelled the blood and the three of them ate that baby mouse in no time at all. They bit off the head, then gnawed into the stomach. The guts looked like porcelain miniatures, but the fish ate them before they separated completely so I never got to see them sink into the water. As I fed them the second mouse, the fish almost jumped out the tank. By then I could see the change in their eyes: no longer flat and empty, now charged with the thick beat of a new electricity. They'd consumed something living, and suddenly their tiny world was no longer closed in by glass walls.

The hallways and rooms in the motel were heavy with the ghosts of its tenants. Mike's room held a twin bed, a mini-fridge, and all of his shitty clothes. There was no kitchen, no bathroom – Mike had to share a single toilet and shower stall with the rest of the derelicts in the motel. There was a nightstand, all flimsy plastic wood and carved-in graffiti, and on it rested three photos: the two sons, a bleeding Jesus, and a young Mike, still with all four limbs, holding up a marlin, his face aglow from holding that big life on a string.

After we met with Mike, we'd go home and smoke the stuff and then usually we'd have sex. Adam liked to tie me up and hit me with his hands, sometimes a belt, sometimes a crop we'd bought at the pet supply store – because crops meant for horses were cheaper than those meant for people – before fucking me. This was the only kind of sex I could manage anymore; the old soft kind left me feeling both bored and alone. When we tried to fuck normal, always on Adam's volition, I'd lay silent, flat on my back, Adam's chest heaving over me, as he looked at my face while I stared at the fish in the tank that illuminated the room from the foot of our bed. The fish's eyes were blank and their mouths opened and closed with nothing coming out. When I looked at them, it seemed like we were the exact same kind of being.

At first it was enough to have my ass turn red, but soon the effectiveness faded and I needed him to bruise me in order to feel any sort of thing at all. One time he slapped me so hard I got a black eye, and the pleasure surged from the weight of his hand. Even looking in the mirror later, watching the bruise that cupped my eye as it waned from blue to yellow in the passing days, made me feel almost like I loved him again, almost like his name was still carved inside my heart. But the black eye scared Adam off. Said he was a nice Catholic boy; nice Catholic boys don't beat their women like that, even if and when they ask for it. I'd wanted to point out the incongruity, that nice Catholic boys don't smoke drugs like these either, but sometimes when you're

Glass, Distilled

I started using meth the way most people do: one day our dealer was out of everything else. Things were different after that. We only ever did meth anymore. Adam was in charge of how and when we got high. Not having my own drugs bothered me sometimes, but not enough to figure out how to make the money to get my own. Most days, seemed good enough to have someone so obsessed with me that he'd pay for this life. He must have thought if he kept me high, I might love him in return. But things had changed, and I wasn't sure he meant much to me anymore.

Our drug dealer Mike was past the acceptable age of someone in his line of work. He lived in a pay-by-the-month motel down the street. Bald, overweight, and a diabetic amputee. To get the drugs, we had to sit in his room and listen to stories about his pathetic life. He enlisted in the navy at the age of seventeen, got kicked out thirteen years later for the habit he'd picked up. It was unclear whether it was the diabetes, the drugs, or the war that caused the loss of his arm. He waved the stump, like it still ended in a hand, as he told us how he got married to a Taiwanese chick overseas. How in quick succession she gave birth to two sons, then asked for divorce the same month she got naturalized. He hadn't seen his sons in six years now. Mike always talked about how he was getting his kids back soon, but of course soon never came because soon never does. As he said this, his face went blank and he covered his stump with his one good hand, in a way that almost eclipsed the deformity.

Mike and Adam always talked about fish. Mike liked both snorkeling and fishing, back when his body was whole and the sadness hadn't yet crept in, back when he was still a young man and in the navy. Adam had a huge tank of fresh waters – cichlids, three puffers, and an eel. He'd picked up the hobby around the same time my emotions slipped away. Both little things that needed to be fed.

your mother is still wearing the same perfume, the same one that, when you smell it on strange women in the subway, still makes you think of coming home from school to the lights off and the blinds drawn and that weird burnt chemical smell heavy in the air.

She called me today. It's been six years since we first "reunited," and I have to give it to her – she tries. Sometimes I can hear the questions in between her silences on the phone: *Why won't you forgive me?* But I don't have to worry. I know she's too afraid to ask.

thin-skinned like chicken meat, one bicep adorned with a tattooed rose. His teeth were dark and small like my mother's.

It was Chuck who got me out of there. Right when my mother's looks really started to spiral, right when her cheeks began to sink into her face. He was sleeping there too often, and where he slept, his clients followed. Can't raise a little girl in a crack house. I wasn't even sad when I left because they let me bring my stuffed cat and Ninja Turtle toothbrush.

I was twenty-three when my mother cleaned up. The social workers and therapists – they all told me I should talk to her. Forgiveness leads to healing, they said, and I agreed.

Like them, I wanted to see things between us sewn up. I was mature enough to know that the first phone call might be filtered through awkward pauses, and it was. I went to the resulting lunch date – at a diner, Formica tables and big dirty windows – fully prepared that some residual anger might sneak up in my chest, and it did. A fist rising up like indigestion from the moment I saw her from across the restaurant, looking sad-eyed into a cup of coffee at a corner booth. She was no longer beautiful. I saw that, and I will admit this is when the fist receded. Now she actually looked like she could be somebody's mother. She was mine.

I thought she wouldn't recognize me, it had been so long. I had it all rehearsed in my head, how I would stand over her and say, *It's me, Mom. It's your daughter*, and she would look confused and surprised. But she saw me and stood up. There were tears in her eyes, and she hugged me tight, and it all felt so Hallmark melodrama it made me squeamish. I tried to not shut down, to not shut her out, to not get cold and steely on the inside; I really wanted to give it all a fair chance. But it's hard when

The phone in the kitchen rang less. My mother was home more. Her front two teeth were grey, hiding in shadows. The dates, the calls, the jobs, the absences: the duration between them all grew wider. The front teeth's vigor returned; they glowed yellow like streetlamps, but it was a tricky surge and didn't last long. Soon they shrank, grew dark and withered.

You might think that because my mother was home more, because she had more time for me, the love she shared with me would grow. But it was like her teeth. What was once only faintly flawed became something dark and rotting. I missed school a lot then. What made it worse was I was rarely allowed to go into the kitchen, where she was. Where she sat with her cigarettes, glass and paper, always something being drawn to her mouth that wasn't me.

The phone began ringing again. I thought this was good, except she kept hanging up without speaking. Ring-bang, ring-bang. I counted them while I watched the TV. Thirty-six. Thirty-six rings til she picked up the phone. Jesus fucking Christ, what is it, she yelled. My kid is trying to sleep.

The digital clock read 6:23. It was light out.

I crept into the doorway of the kitchen, low so she wouldn't see. She cradled the phone on her neck, lit one of her long white cigarettes. She exhaled through the black gap of her mouth. That could work, she said to the phone.

Chuck was over a lot now. That's what he told me to call him. He slept in my mother's bed sometimes, snoring real low and rumbly, but that, of course, wasn't as bad as the other noises that slid under the door. Chuck's muscles bulged in odd places and his arms and chest seemed

She would take me to the magazine stands whenever a photo she had been in was published. Sometimes she'd be out all night, and come in with a slam of the door, and then she'd wake me up and make me put on my sneakers. I could feel her excitement as she took my hand and pulled me into the street. It's so bright! she shrilled in my ear, once we were on the sidewalk. We went down the street, down the blocks where the concrete sparkled like fairies. I looked up at my mother, her straightened, highlighted hair, its ends in tangles, her eyes sooty with eyeliner, the faint lines settling in like dust around her mouth.

At the newsstand my mother bought me candy. She slit open the package and poured some into my hand, and I ate them as she tore through the pages of the magazine. The bright colors of the candy in my hand and then in my mouth were too vivid to belong there, but my mother had given them to me so I ate them anyway. They were chewy and stuck to my teeth.

Here it is, she said, and then handed me the magazine. A close-up of her face. It looked like my mother but it didn't. She was wearing all black; her hair hung down around her, smooth, golden, and liquid. Her mouth was open, and her teeth, underneath her parted pink lips, looked sharp and scary. Feline.

Is that you? I said, and pointed to the lady in the magazine. I looked up at my mother, dirty and buzzing in the bright morning light. Two images, the same but different, like looking into a smear-stained mirror.

Yes, of course it's me, she said, Give me that. She ripped the magazine from my hands, closed it shut so fast it made a slapping sound, and slid it into her purse.

Things really began to slip once her teeth started getting fucked up.

happening at the right time or would stay standing up. My mother would not sleep, she would bake for me, cookies and pies, she would sew up the holes in my clothes, make me stuffed teddy bears, bring home sparkly things from photo shoots for me to play with. Always laughing and singing through her shiny white teeth. We went to the parks at dawn and had picnics, jelly sandwiches with the crusts cut off. The leaves on the trees were new and green and so impossibly small like the toys of dolls; the pink lemonade in my wax cup was the same color as the edges of brightening sky. Pinkies up! my mother said, sticking her finger and elbow up and out. I tried to imitate her and failed – holding the cup was pretty much the pinnacle of my motor skills – and she laughed and tickled my stomach, spilling lemonade on my dress, but my dress was pink too and my mother was happy so a little bit of juice didn't matter.

And then she slept, she cried, her mouth was a slit, I was hungry and so I poured myself cereal but I spilled the milk and then ran into the street for fear my mother would hit me. She would hit me. Three hours later, my mother retrieved me, her face puffy and tear-stained but smiling, from Mrs. Jenkins's down the hall. She took me by the hand, told me how worried she was. Mrs. Jenkins clucked her tongue, said how silly children were, gave a sympathetic look to my mother. Then my mother took me across the hall, closed the door, turned on the record player, Jane's Addiction (I still hate that band), and then she hit me. First she was just thwacking me on my thighs and butt, this was spanking and she said it was okay, Perry Farrell was whining about summertime, but I started to cry, she turned up the music and then she hit me across the mouth. *Shut up*, she said to me, *Shut up, you ugly little brat.* My lip began to bleed and then swell. I wasn't allowed to go to school for a week, even though my mother was still getting gigs then and gone most days. All week, the TV was my babysitter.

The Sharpest Part of Her

My mother had been clean for most of her pregnancy so no one suspected what was to come. True, no family had come while she was in labor, or even after I was born. No father, either. But it was New York, it was 1982, and this was common enough.

It took three days, she told me. Three days of listening to me scream. I didn't shut up, except to sleep, and those intervals were not enough for her. She held me, she fed me, she rocked me, she sang – she did everything she was supposed to – yet all I did was scream.

I suppose that's why there should be two parents, she said, one to relieve the other to save them both from going nuts.

But there weren't two parents; there was only her. My father may have been a photographer, a club promoter, or another model, and it didn't matter which, because each of the potential liaisons-turned-sperm donors were 'scumbags' and 'idiots.'

Not my mother, of course. My mother, the blond beauty, was now a young single mother, and she couldn't handle the pressure. Less than seventy-two hours after she left the hospital, her old coke dealer was on the phone. I needed to get my figure back, she told me, I needed to find some joy.

Finding joy– it's always stunned me how little her justifications made sense. But I guess the strangest part of the whole situation was that she told me at all.

Therapists have looked at me, eyes wet and round, and said that growing up in a household like mine must have not felt that strange because it was all I knew. I can't say this was true for me, because I do remember the pliancy of things, how nothing ever felt like it was me, but still, it was a pretty shitty thing for her to do.

Oh, but I didn't mean for it to go like this. This story was supposed to be them: the couple, two people, symmetrical, no piece of me. But with every breath and every step, I find myself more entwined with them. We are braided around each other like snakes.

Some days I don't wake up till the sun's going down and my role in things weighs down so darkly it near chokes me.

Anyway. Here is the story of the two of them, the short version. He started heroin and then quit. They got together. They fought a lot. They broke up. She started shooting. They got back together. He started shooting again. They both quit. They broke up. They started and stopped many more times, both with the drugs and each other. Eventually they realized that no matter what they would still be unhappy, and this made them perfect for each other. They were soulmates now. They quit doing drugs for a long time, and stayed unhappy and in love. They lived, and when they were very old they started shooting again, for no reason at all. And then they died.

Heroin Story

The heroin story I know best is about a couple. I met the boy a long time ago. He told me he was single but that was a lie. We slept together for a while, off and on, despite his unsingleness. We fought a lot and hated each other sometimes, until one day I looked at him and realized he had become my very close friend. Once I smoked some DMT because someone gave it to me, and it made me giggle and I couldn't stand up from the bed I was sitting on. I had a dream, and in the dream I was a lot older, I knew I had aged because my skin felt light like paper but the inside of me was solid and dark. The sun was low in the sky and thick yellow like tree sap, that gorgeous time of day right before the sun begins to set. I was with the boy and he was older too, a man now, and we were married; there were vines growing up the fence and the leaves were buzzing with new growth and his skin was warm under my fingers as I kissed him. I looked in his eyes, the man in the dream, and couldn't believe that I had known, and hated, and loved this person for so long. In him I could see who I was, who I had been.

But the problem with DMT is it makes you dream and the dream seems so real, but it lasts so short and goes away so fast. I was back in the bedroom and the light dragged trails.

I hadn't known the girl as long. The boy had to wait for us to be just friends before he could introduce me to her, because he'd been the girl's the entire time we were sleeping together, plus a year or two before that. It turned out that when I'd met him she'd recently smashed out his car windows with her bare fists, and also given him genital warts. She told me later, much later when we too were friends, that she'd known she had warts but she wanted to keep it a secret from him, just to have one, something that was not his but would be soon, like a baby. She cut them off (there were three, triplets) with a pair of manicure scissors and taped them in her journal like they were old scabs. When he asked her what the cuts were from she said she was fucked up and shaving. She said it was a hard spot to shave. He didn't pass the genital warts on to

We fell into a state of nothingness after that. I spent the days after the appointment staring through the bedroom window, out at our view of the alley. Sometimes the haze would turn the sky scarlet at sunset and the birds would perch on the power lines in blackened silhouettes, but usually I must admit that I was staring at nothing at all. He would come home from work and find me there, silent and smelling of blood. He tried to kiss me, on my cheek, on my forehead, turning my face toward his and placing his mouth over mine, silently demanding I kiss back, but it was always him kissing me, and me just being there.

hearted and blanched. He went to work and constructed code, I waited tables and collected tips, sometimes I'd wake up at dawn and find myself tangled in his arms, one of my yellow hairs stuck to his eyebrow. We got nosebleeds. We made lasagna. I got pregnant.

He had told me he was sterile, that his stepfather had thrown a can of beans at his nuts when he was nine. I asked what kind and he said, "Refried," so we did it without a condom and had been doing so ever since. He was good enough to not ask if it was really his. I was dumb enough to not wonder if he'd been lying all along.

I was taking a night class, English, at the community college. Sometimes I'd get all the way to campus only to keep on driving, ditching class to eat Taco Bell. On the occasions I did make it into the classroom, I usually fell asleep on my desk, the teacher's voice a bland lullaby. Pregnancy turned me into a baby myself—all I wanted was to eat and sleep. I'd come home from class and collapse on the bed, and sometimes my boyfriend would hold me. "My babies," he'd say, stroking my hair.

We saved up the money for the abortion by the second month. I hadn't wanted one, because I liked feeling it grow, but he convinced me that this was unwise. Only when we got to Planned Parenthood, the doctor said there was no heartbeat. She examined me and, with her gloved, lubricated fingers still inside, said I must have expelled it on my own. The word "expelled" made me feel like a snake, like something that had slipped out of its own skin.

He, strangely enough, was mad at me. "How could you not notice something like that falling out?" Like he thought there'd be a bloody baby squirming in the toilet, and I was too stupid to pluck it from the water.

Reduction

This was the old days, back when you could go down to Tijuana without a passport. It started with us lying on my bed and snorting ketamine. He had a co-worker with a sick grandmother who lived down there; the co-worker would visit and come back with a few vials of the stuff. My not-yet-boyfriend and I cooked one down in the kitchen of my shitty little studio, pouring it into the previously unused glass casserole dish my mom had given me to make lasagna. "Lasagnas are nutritious," she had said, "and they freeze well." We added a dash of vanilla and cooked it for twenty minutes on low, like baking cookies. The crystals formed pale yellow, and once we had them chopped up and snorted, the drip tasted like chemicals and candy.

He wasn't much besides his job—a programmer, Linux—but I didn't know that yet. Hard to have foresight when you're spending nights on your back with the room throbbing inside your ears, when your version of an activity is clumsy fucking. It all sounds so stupid and misguided, one giant act of folly, us beginning our relationship like that.

But we'd lay on my sheets and sweat and not move, and I'd look at him, I'd look right into him, and I knew we were cut from the same sheer cloth. Apart, on our own, we were pale and flimsy, but on top of each other we gained shape, could almost stand straight up. It made sense, and it wasn't just the drugs.

Three weeks in, and he brought over his laptop and all his clothes. He had lived with his boss, who was a Christian, and spending nights alone made him feel suicidal. We could never sleep, and the early mornings were spent staring at our computer screens like they were mirrors, like if we looked hard enough we could find the outline of ourselves.

The grandmother in Tijuana died, so we stopped baking and did coke instead. Sometimes we argued, but our words were always half-

XI

There are two more bus trips and hotel rooms. Each trip goes pretty much the same. Each morning you wake up alone and he's at the casinos, and he never picks up his cell phone and it all makes you feel so helpless and pale and when you ride back to the city there's never anything to say. Spring is coming, and coat check season will be over soon.

XII

You leave your laptop open on the couch and go get a haircut. While you're gone, your boyfriend reads your messages. The worst one is the most recent.

i love my boyfriend but i think i might be starting to love you too

You have no idea why you even typed that.

There is a fight. In it, you become single and homeless. In the morning, you call Jonathan and you are crying and you tell him the truth, which is that your heart is destroyed. You want to tell him it's his fault, but it isn't – this was all broken by you.

He tells you to pack your things and take the train up to 59th and Lexington. You can live with him. You won't even have to work. Something in the way he's phrasing things tells you this is exactly what he wanted all along.

You think about it, what it would be like to live in Manhattan, how there would be dinners out and manicures, jewelry and fancy shoes. You'd sleep til noon, every day. You'd sit at the window, and stare down at lights that looked like Oz, and you'd be there, trapped and pretty, a golden life charmed, but one not meant for a girl like you.

IX

In Atlantic City, he wants to play poker and have you sit by his side. You think about all the girls that came before you, five and ten years under your age, and how they all probably said yes, but watching men fling around money sounds boring so you refuse. You've never been interested in acting like anyone's trophy – which is one reason why he likes you. You're older so you do what you want.

Instead, you go straight to the room. It is nothing fancy, and for a moment you are disappointed. But then he kisses you hard, and lowers you onto the bed, and reaches up your skirt and pulls down your thong without pause and without asking. For the second time that night he smiles, and then he enters you.

X

Afterwards, you stare up at the ceiling, naked, no covers over your body.

He pulls you into his chest, and he smells entirely unfamiliar.

You ask Jonathan to tell you a story, a request you used to ask your boyfriend when it was late but you still couldn't sleep. Your boyfriend always said no, his excuse being he has no way with words, so you stopped asking.

Jonathan is a different man. He strokes your hair, and tells you about the homeless people on the streets of Miami Beach, and how he paid them in malt liquor to do security at his club. You close your eyes, and you smile, and soon you are asleep. When you wake, Jonathan is gone, busy losing his money at the casinos. He comes back in a very bad mood. The afternoon bus ride home is quiet and sullen, too bright, and there are no city fairy tales on the way.

you aren't actually angry.

In the cab home, your friend asks, "What's going on with you and Jonathan?"

"Nothing," you say, and because you're bad at lying you stare out the window.

VII

On Sunday night, you pack a bag and ride to Port Authority. You're wearing a black dress and high boots with fishnets because that's what he told you to wear, and you are wicked. He's waiting for you outside like he said he'd be, smoking his Marlboro Reds. He smiles when he sees you. He never smiles. It is weird to see him happy.

VIII

You sit in the back of the bus. The floor lights are purple, and people are already slumped and sleeping against the windows. The lights of Lincoln Tunnel go by so fast that it feels like a zoetrope. You go underground as yourself, and as the lights flick by you spin into a cheater.

It is late and the world is quiet and New Jersey looks pretty in the dark. You ask Jonathan to tell you about being a teenager in New York in the eighties. He tells you it was a different city, with all that crime. He tells you about sitting in the back of CBGBs. He tells you the kids at the clubs would wear lace and eyeliner and dance to Siouxsie Sioux, and everyone was brilliant and fabulous, and there was no bottle service or fake lines out front. His voice is soft and it feels like he is speaking fairy tales. You look out the window into the darkness, and your secret is inside you and you feel sordid but also happy and you think to yourself, this is my life.

Around the corner on Delancey, and he is waiting for you in the back of a black car. You get in. He takes you to breakfast. You order waffles, with whipped cream and strawberries, but are too nervous to eat much. He looks old in the diner light, which brings out the bags under his eyes. But the irises are very blue, and his lips look soft.

He kisses you for the first time in front of that diner. It is cold, and you forgot your gloves, and the puffs of both your breaths intermingle in clouds. He gives you a twenty to take a cab home.

Your boyfriend stirs in his sleep as you enter the bedroom. He is shirtless and illuminated by the hall light. "I tried to stay up for you," he says, his voice thick with sleep. "What time is it?"

"Six," you say, although it's seven, and the lie worms in your gut. "Some of us got breakfast."

After you take off your make-up and clothes, you get in bed next to him. His heart beats steady and strong. You wrap your arms around him and whisper *I love you* into his ear, and you mean it so much you start to cry.

V

Your boyfriend takes a long weekend upstate, with his friend who has a recording studio in the shed. You can't go because you have work.

VI

On Saturday, you stand in the basement again, waiting for your friend. Jonathan is next to you, talking about nothing in a low voice. He stands too close. You're worried someone will see so you pull away, but he moves in again and cups your ass in his hands. You swear at him, but

III

Christmas happens. You go to your boyfriend's home for the second year in a row and his parents have a fire lit and it is snowing and they are happy to see you. The two of you sleep in his childhood bed and you feel so safe in his arms and they are around you like a blanket but all you want to do is go outside so you can shiver. There is something deeply wrong at your core and you know it and have always known it but he doesn't see it yet.

IV

In the new year, you wait in the basement, which is dark and smelly because this is the floor where the clientele get the freakiest. Apparently it is not unusual to watch some girl get fingerbanged on the dance floor. At least that's what the bartenders say.

It is five AM. You have four hundred dollars rolled up, in the zippered part of your pocketbook. You sip a whiskey and ginger and watch yourself in the mirror behind the bar. Your make-up and hair are still perfect, and you look slinky and you could totally pass for twenty-two.

The idea is you are waiting to take a car back to Brooklyn with your friend, a bartender who's still busy cashing out. The truth is you are waiting for the right time to slip away with the owner. His name is Jonathan.

"How much longer?" you say to your friend as she counts the bills under her breath. "I'm getting really tired."

"I haven't added the tips yet." This means she won't be ready for another thirty minutes, at least, which is perfect. She starts back at one, because you made her lose count. You finish your drink and tell her you'll just go home alone.

The Other Kind of Magic

I

You work in a nightclub, in coat check. The club is three stories, and well drinks are twelve dollars. This is in Manhattan, right near the Williamsburg Bridge. The coat check is on the top floor, which is closed in by a glass ceiling. The lights on the bridge look like they are there specifically to impress all the girls in their tight neon dresses and all the boys in their polo shirts, as they get fucked up on bottle service and molly and sing along to that Jay-Z song.

The coat check job is three nights a week, Thursday through Saturday. You make more in a night at this job than you do in two weeks at your "real" job, which is adjuncting English. To do *that* job, you need an advanced degree. To do *this* job, you need to put on a lot of make-up and a slutty outfit and look younger than your twenty-nine years. Nothing adds up in New York, and you like that.

One of the owners has a thing for you. He stands there and stares at you from the end of the hallway, wearing his dark velvet suits. He's mean to everyone, swearing and brooding, but for you he brings cupcakes from the kitchen. You smoke together on the deck when it's slow. He tells you about his girlfriend, who is seven years younger than you and covered in tattoos. They fight a lot. You ask him if they tell each other 'I love you' and he says yes, but it's just something he says. He asks you if you do the same with your boyfriend, and you say yes, but you actually mean it. You tell him how nice your boyfriend is, how smart and funny and talented. You tell him how happy you are together and how it's assumed you'll marry, but even you hear the catch in your voice. It starts to rain, and the cabs drive by in whispers.

II

The tattooed girl and the owner break up. You and your boyfriend stay together.

In the kitchen before dinner one night, it turned out I'd had too much and I fainted. One moment I had my elbows on the counter and the next I was a sloppy puddle on the floor. I'd hit the tile smack on my cheekbone. In the morning I had a black eye. "Looks like you talked back," he joked. I pretended to laugh, but really I was thinking about how his dumb jokes made me sick.

Our last night together, and we went to the sex shop to buy whippets. I hadn't done those things since I was fifteen. We went out on the patio and sat in the chairs, our big pint glasses forming rings on the old wooden planks of the deck. The empty cartridges made a pile at our feet, silver and glinting spent bombs. The iciness of the gas brought blisters to our fingers. And our thoughts – they stilled before they burst, and then we laughed, and then we laughed.

It smelled like gasoline because of the airport, and looked nothing at all like the beach. But if I sucked enough nitrous and shook my head the right way, I could trick myself into thinking the roar of the jets was that of the waves, and the lights on the landing strip were, in fact, stars.

Fuck California

That was the summer the waters in the lagoon swelled, and the gnats and mosquitoes swarmed in black clouds. We would sit on the beach in his rusty lawn chairs, the nylon threads turning white before snapping. We drank cases of beer, first cold and then no longer cold and then warm, out of cans hidden in paper bags, and the bug bites popped red on our heels. The day turned into night, and we rolled from the chairs onto the sand, not really minding the bugs, and I whispered to him, "I love you," for the very first time, and I meant it.

I thought I meant it.

The days grew shorter and the mosquito bites healed. That was the winter the kelp uprooted itself, splaying on the sand in rusty, rotting piles, making the beach stink of death. We went down there one night, hopeful, but I could only stand it for ten minutes. Right before we left – he didn't want us to go – I said to him, "It just seems like the ocean is trying to get at us," and he smiled at me like I was a morbid and silly child. He was one of those that came here from somewhere else, and saw everything as great, waking just about every day to declare it a beautiful morning. Fuck California, I said under my breath. And also: fuck you.

We took his lawn chairs back where they came from, to the deck at his house, where we could see a little of downtown and the bay, which was polluted, but mostly we were looking at the airport. This was also the winter I couldn't get warm. The sea air dug into my bones, it seemed, and wouldn't get out – there really was no other explanation. My skin was thinner, more transparent, than before, and my veins seemed much more blue; my arms and chest looked like maps, maps with a whole lot of rivers. I drank to melt away the chill. I couldn't tell you why he drank, all I know was he did it too.

BLACK CLOUD

for Scott

TABLE OF CONTENTS

Fanzine

- "Recurring Intrusive Thoughts" – *The Lazy Fascist Review*; NY Tyrant
- "Flame War," "Contemporary Guilt" – Two Serious Ladies
- "Sexy Terrorist," "Sexy Terrorist Pt. 2," – The Heavy Contortionists
- "On the Construction Site Behind My House," "Fur Trade," "The Scenic Route" – Shabby Doll House
- "The Name of This Poem is a Picture" – The Ampersand Review
- "Long Distance Love Poem," "2013 Poem From a 1992 Story" – *The Bushwick Review*
- "But Do You Love Me," "All I'm Asking for is Perfection" – The Quietus
- "That Was Then, This is Now," "Hot New Diet Tip" – Goblin Reservation
- "Anxiety Attacks" – Western Beefs of North America
- "The Other Kind of Magic" – Vol. 1 Brooklyn
- "Heroin Story" – Electric Literature's The Outlet
- "The Sharpest Part of Her" – *Pear Noir!*
- "Hurricane Season" – *New Ohio Review*
- "Mental Illness on a Weekday" – Negative Suck
- "Here is a Ghost Story" – *Black Candies: See Through*
- "Grunion Run" – Everyday Genius

Acknowledgments

Thank you, Leza and Christoph, for giving these books a second life.
Thank you to Michael J. Seidlinger at CCM, Emily Gould and Ruth Curry at Emily Books, Cameron Pierce and Rose O'Keefe at Lazy Fascist/Eraserhead, Claudia Apablaza at Los Libros de la Mujer Rota, Martin Brinkmann, and MaroVerlag for publishing *Black Cloud* and *Witch Hunt* in their original forms.

A line in "Leo Queen" is plagiarized from Joan Didion's *A Book of Common Prayer* (not a good book).

Thank you to Monika Woods for your wisdom and guidance.

Thank you to Scott for everything. This has been the best decade of my life.

Thank you to the following publications and their editors for publishing these stories and poems:

- "The Triangle Shirtwaist Fire of 1911" – *Southwest Review*
- "David Foster Wallace's Rock Idol Was Axl Rose," "Emotional Truth" – Dark Fucking Wizard
- "Who is Responsible for My Emotional Problems?," "And One More for the Dog Parade," "The Bodies That Fail Us," "Another Nature Poem," "Things My Students Have Emailed Me in the Past Couple Weeks," "Self-Knowledge is the Key to Something," "How to Upset a Californian," "Just the Tip," "Who Says That Fast Food Can't Bring A Spiritual Awakening," "Top 10 Greatest Feels," "Reduction" – Hobart
- "God Poem II," "God Poem III" – *Witchcraft Magazine*, issue 5
- "Flame War," "Paragard," "Sexy Terrorist, Part II" – *Through Clenched Teeth*
- "Letters to Ex-Lovers" – Nerve
- "Astral Project My Pussy," "29th Street, Manhattan," "Win Friends, Influence People," "All the Bad News in 2014," "True Story" –

photo by Saja Montague.

Juliet Escoria

Juliet Escoria is the author of the story collection *You Are the Snake* (forthcoming from Soft Skull in 2024) and *Juliet the Maniac* (Melville House, May 2019). Her first two books, *Black Cloud* and *Witch Hunt*, were previously published by Civil Coping Mechanisms and Lazy Fascist Press, respectively. Her writing can be found in places like Tyrant, VICE, Hotel, and the New York Times, and has been translated into many languages. She was born in Australia, raised in San Diego, and currently lives in West Virginia.

Praise For Juliet Escoria

"Escoria's debut short story collection is a brazen admission of the pains of reality in a time when pretending to be happy – to make light of your sadness – is easier than ever. The tone is a combination of Denis Johnson and Joan Didion, and although the stories are focused on drugs (and a wide variety of), Escoria never uses them gratuitously. Rather, each story is a dose of potent insight on the motivations and experiences of users both active and struggling-to-be former."

—Lauren Oyler, Dazed

"Unrelenting, violent, often scary: Juliet Escoria's debut collection of stories will likely have you begging and crying for salvation a few pages in. She's just that good."

—Jason Diamond, Flavorwire

"Simply riveting and raw."

—Lindsay Hunter, FSG blog

"These stories are uniformly effective; they veer at you in unexpected ways and devastate, sometimes quietly and sometimes brutally."

—Tobias Carroll, Vol. 1 Brooklyn

"[U]sing sparse and elegant prose, Escoria makes the reader feel. Moreover, even when what the reader feels is terrible and frightening, Escoria finds a way to make it beautiful. These are powerful stories. Read them and be moved."

—David S. Atkinson, Lit Hub

"For fans of Ottessa Moshfegh, *Juliet the Maniac* is a worthy new entry in that pantheon of deconstruction... Dazzling."

—New York Times Book Review

Juliet Escoria

BLACK CLOUD
& WITCH HUNT

NEW AND SELECTED WORKS

Cover art and interior by Joel Amat Güell
joelamatguell.com | *@joelamatguell*

ISBN: 9781955904933

Troy, NY
CLASH Books
clashbooks.com

@clashbooks @clashbooks /clashbooks

Email: clashmediabooks@gmail.com

CLASH
FICTION